CLASH OF CLEATS

BILL SUMMERS

FULL SUN PRESS

Clash of Cleats

FULL SUN PRESS
Basking Ridge, New Jersey

www.billsummersbooks.com

CHAPTER 1
NEW KID AT TRYOUTS

AYLIGHT WAS FADING AWAY ON **Max Miles**. His tryout was almost over. He had to do something big, and he had to do it now.

Thirty yards from goal, Max clipped the ball off his foe's boot. His eyes up, he saw a teammate racing down the flank. Max lofted the ball toward the corner and bolted for the goal. As he dashed into the box he saw the cross sailing in, and he knew he had only one chance. *Here goes – diving header.*

Springing off the balls of his feet, Max flew like a dart. His forehead met the ball, and then his chin met the grass. Max saw the ball sizzle past the stunned keeper and snap the strings. Scrambling up, he felt his chest go *boom-boom-boom*, that special drumbeat that followed every goal. As he jogged back up the field, Max could feel every eye on him.

A short kid with stringy blond hair ran up to Max. "Cool shot!" yelled Fivehead Cannon. "How'd you do that?"

"Closed my eyes and hoped for a miracle," Max replied. He turned, and bumped shoulders with the kid who had marked him all game. "That shot *was* a miracle," Red Peters snapped. "You'll never do that again."

Max felt Red's cold eyes slicing into him. The whistle blew. "Bring it in, boys," called out Jack Pepper, coach of the Thunder, an under-twelve travel team in Chelsea, Pennsylvania. Sixteen boys jogged toward the sideline. Fifteen were already on the Thunder – everyone but Max. This was his tryout, his chance to make the team after moving from Liverpool, New Jersey.

As Max reached the bench, one question bounced in his head: *Did I do enough to make it?* Max edged to the outside of the huddle, his heart thumping hard. Coach ran a hand over the dark bristles sticking straight off his head. "Okay, boys, remind me what team won our league last year?"

"Thunder!" the boys shouted.

Coach nodded. "That's right, and that means we go into this season with a bullseye on our backs. Are we gonna let another team take our crown?"

"No!" the boys hollered.

Coach smiled. "You got that right. See you next week."

The boys grabbed their bags and walked off, but Max froze. *Do I ask Coach if I made it?* When Coach stepped away and began to stuff balls into his bag, Max turned for the lot.

"Wait up, Max," Coach called.

Max froze. Coach Pepper walked over and fixed his dark eyes on him. "Thanks for trying out, I'll call you tonight."

"Sounds good, Coach."

Max gave Coach his phone number and email address and trotted off. Fivehead ran up to him. "Mack, you're awesome. You'll make the team, for sure."

Max smiled. "Thanks. By the way, my name's Max."

Fivehead bounced a hand off his forehead. "Got it, Max. I'm Wesley, but everyone calls me, 'Fivehead.'"

"Cool nickname, how'd you get it?"

Before Fivehead could answer, Red's voice filled the air. "Get over here, Fivehead!"

Fivehead tossed his head back, his hair swishing around his ears. "Tell ya about my name later, see ya."

Max swung his eyes to Red, standing by a car, glaring at Fivehead. *That Red kid is trouble, I can feel it in my bones.* Max spotted his mom's car. He jogged over and got in. "How'd it go?" she asked.

"These guys can play, Mom. They're way better than my team in Liverpool."

"Think you'll make it?" she asked.

"Not sure, Coach said he'd call me tonight."

Mrs. Miles drove off. "I watched the last ten minutes. Your diving header was awesome."

"Thanks. Bit my tongue, check it out." Max stuck out his tongue, but his mom didn't bother to look. She tucked a few strands of thick red hair behind her ear. "You had some open shots, but you passed instead."

Max tossed his head back. "You want me to hog the ball at my tryout?"

"Just sayin'. Hey, that tall boy you were marking, he's pretty good."

"That's Red Peters, the captain."

"That's wild," his mom said. "You're both tall, red-haired center-midfielders."

"Kid kept yankin' my arm, even stepped on my toes a few times," Max whined. "Then he got in my face after my diving header. Maybe he's worried cuz I play his position, and I just schooled him."

"There's one rascal on every team, Max."

"One?" Max snapped. "This Eddie kid kept tryin' to cut me down."

Mrs. Miles shot Max a doubtful look. "Maybe you just imagined it."

"I know when a guy tries to trip me," Max shot back. He looked out the window, his thoughts racing back to Liverpool. "I can't believe we moved here, moved away from all my friends."

"You'll make new friends on this team," his mom said.

"Yeah, like Red and Eddie," Max volleyed. "Plus, I gotta go to sixth grade in a new school."

"It's the first year of middle school," she replied. "It'll be a fresh start for everyone."

"Nice try, Mom. You know I'll be the only new kid."

Max stuck in his earphones for the rest of the

ride home. A bit later he was standing in the shower, replaying his diving header. *I scored a nice goal, but maybe Mom's right. What if I had banged in a few more?* His shower done, Max toweled off and put on shorts and a T-shirt. He paced across his cocoa-colored carpet, his eyes darting to the digital clock on his desk. 5:53. *Seems like every minute lasts an hour. Coach Pepper better call soon, or I'm gonna wear a hole in this carpet.*

"Dinner's ready!" called his mom. Max grabbed his phone and scooted downstairs. He joined his parents and his thirteen-year-old sister, Betsy, at the kitchen table. Betsy looked at Max.

"How'd your tryout go?" she asked.

"One kid left his fingerprints all over my arms, but I did okay," Max replied. "I'll find out tonight if I made it."

Max squirted a wavy line of mustard on his hot dog. He was about to take his first bite when his phone dinged. Max looked at his mom. She nodded, and he snatched his phone and scurried into the mud room.

"Hello," Max said.

"Max, Coach Pepper here. Welcome to the Thunder!"

Max felt a bolt of joy rocket through him. "Coach, that's awesome!"

"I know you'll do great things on the Thunder, Max. I'll send out an email to let everyone know. Our schedule will be attached."

Max thanked Coach and clicked off. He stepped back into the kitchen. "I made it!"

"Way to go, Max!" Mr. Miles shouted. Max hugged his parents and high-fived with Betsy.

"I knew you'd make it, bro," Betsy said. "You'll be the best player on the Thunder."

Later that night, Max got the email from Coach Pepper. He read it and jabbed a fist at his ceiling. Minutes later, he was tapping a tennis ball across his carpet when his phone beeped. It was another email, with the subject 'Thunder Soccer.' He opened it.

"No one on the Thunder wants you. Don't even THINK about joining our team."

"Mom, come here!" Max called. Mrs. Miles raced up the stairs, and Max gave her the phone.

"Read that." She read the message. "This is crazy, Max. Who would do such a thing?"

Max booted his tennis ball into the wall. "Bet it's Red Peters."

"I'm calling Coach Pepper."

"No, Mom, I'll look like a wimp."

Max flopped on his bed. "The Thunder's been together forever. They're league champs. They don't need me, it's like I'm butting in. Maybe I should look for another team."

Mrs. Miles sat. "Max, you're a great player. You need to play for the best team."

"But some guys don't like me. You should see Red's eyes. It's like they burn right through me."

His mom crossed her arms. "Look, you've had a long day, time for bed."

A bit later Max climbed into bed. He rolled over, his eyes landing on the picture on his windowsill. It showed Max on his first soccer team, standing next to his first coach, his mom. Mrs. Miles had played soccer in college, on a full scholarship. She was an All-American striker. She was going to turn pro, until she tore ligaments in her right knee, for the third and final time.

Max thought about his mom's words. *You had some open shots, but you passed instead.* Max blew out a sigh. *That's my mom. Whatever I do, it's not quite good enough.* Exhausted from his tryout, Max drifted off, his light still on.

When Max woke the next morning, the email rattled in his head. He grabbed his phone, read the message again, and hit '*delete.*' *This is creepy. Back in Liverpool, no one treated me like this.*

Max pulled back his window shade and eyed his new backyard. It was the same size as his old yard, but it looked nothing like it. There was no 'Square,' the mini-soccer field covered with cleat marks. No goals. No friends. But he did see one thing he didn't have in Liverpool. Yellow weeds sprouting up everywhere, some white and purple ones mixed in. Max shook his head. *I had the best yard in Liverpool. Here, I got a weed garden. Purple weeds, who knew?*

Max heard the clatter of pans in the kitchen. He went downstairs and found his dad making pancake batter.

"Morning, Max," Mr. Miles said. "You want strawberry or blueberry?"

"Strawberry, I guess," Max mumbled.

Mr. Miles eyed his son. "Max, you okay?"

"I miss our yard in Liverpool, Dad. I mean, look out back. We got more weeds than grass."

"Don't worry, we'll whip this yard into another Square. The goals are coming tomorrow."

Mr. Miles slid three pancakes in front of Max. The bits of strawberry reminded him of Red Peters. *I've met that kid once, and he already haunts me.* As Max poured out a pool of syrup, his mom walked in. "So, Max, I just got a call from our neighbor, Lori Cannon. Their son Wesley plays for Thunder, you met him at your tryout. They asked us to come over later."

Max perked up. "Sounds good. By the way, Wesley goes by, 'Fivehead.'"

"Fivehead?" Mrs. Miles repeated. "How'd he get that nickname?"

"Don't know, but I'll find out."

That afternoon, Max and his mom walked up Hickory Lane to the Cannons' house. A woman answered the doorbell. "Welcome to the neighborhood!" Mrs. Cannon bellowed. Her curly blond hair reminded Max of Fivehead. She eyed Max. "Wesley said you crushed the tryout, Max. He's in his room, why don't you run up?"

Max smiled as he climbed the stairs. He found Fivehead hanging from his door frame, his legs bent off the floor. "Five more seconds," Fivehead blurted. He held on a bit longer, dropped, and flipped his mop off his forehead. "I hang from there for twenty seconds every day," Fivehead said. "I'm so dang short, gotta do what I can to get taller."

Fivehead waved Max into his room, and they dropped onto the thick gray carpet.

"So, Fivehead, how'd you get your nickname?" Max asked.

"We were playing soccer in the backyard, and I kept heading in goals. My brother's friend said, 'Dude, you got the biggest forehead I ever saw. It's not a forehead, it's a fivehead.' It kinda stuck from there."

"You like it?"

"Seemed weird at first, but I'm used to it."

"Bet you're the only 'Fivehead' in the world."

"Bet you're right. So Max, it's great to have you on the Thunder. With you, we'll be untouchable." Fivehead pulled a scrapbook off his bookcase. Max eyed the cover. 'THUNDER, 2018 LEAGUE CHAMPIONS.' They flipped through until Fivehead stopped at the team photo on the last page. "I'll tell you about the guys you'll be playing around." Fivehead put his finger on an Asian boy who wore his long black hair in a ponytail. "Ben Kwan, left midfielder, team genius. Kid sleeps with an open dictionary on his face."

Max chuckled, and Fivehead pointed at Artie Moss. "Good defender, but bossy. You goof up, he'll howl at the moon."

Fivehead moved to Eddie Hazard. "Kid's a scoring machine, but he's always ticked off about somethin'. Known him for five years, seen him smile twice."

"Eddie kept tripping me at the tryout," Max said.

"Cuz he couldn't keep up with you," Fivehead replied.

Fivehead's finger landed on Red Peters. "Best player in town. Big mouth, big head. When he looks in the mirror, he sees his hero."

Max snorted at that. Finally, Fivehead

pointed at himself. "Watch out for this kid. He's proof that dynamite comes in small packages."

Max smiled. Fivehead stood and grabbed two slips of paper off his desk. "I got two coupons for free ice cream. Wanna ride bikes to Mort's Cone Zone?"

"Sounds great!" Max bounded downstairs and got the okay from his mom. He ran over to his garage, fished out his purple junker, and pedaled up to Fivehead on the sidewalk. Fivehead studied Max's bike.

"Never seen a purple bike, pretty cool."

Max eyed the wide tires on Fivehead's lime green bike. "Serious tires, Fivehead."

Fivehead nodded. "Like I say, better to have a fat tire than a flat tire." Fivehead pointed up the sidewalk. "Follow me, we're takin' the trail, not the tar."

Fivehead built speed, popped a wheelie, and held it for ten yards. Then he cut left onto a tarred path leading into the woods behind his house, Max close behind. They pedaled across a footbridge that ran over a creek and picked up a path covered with wood chips. Max watched two squirrels dart across the path and scurry up the trunk of an oak tree. *I got no clue where I am, but this is pretty cool.*

The boys rode through the woods for a half-mile until they reached a clearing behind a row of shops. Max saw the sign for Mort's, and they wheeled up. He ordered a mint chocolate chip cone, Fivehead chose peanut butter twirl, and they sat at a table outside. As Max tore into his cone, his mind raced to that email. It was eating at him. "So Fivehead, I got an email last night. It said the Thunder doesn't want me."

Fivehead scrunched his face. "That's crazy, who sent it?"

"Nobody signed it."

"Maybe it's Red Peters," Fivehead guessed. "Like my mom says, he's a cherry short of a chocolate sundae."

"He kept grabbing my arm at my tryout, said my header was lucky."

"Red has a wicked temper," Fivehead said. "Last year, some kid kept tripping him. Red elbowed the kid, knocked out two teeth. I can still hear the kid screamin'."

Max felt a chill shoot through him. Fivehead put up a hand. "Don't worry, Coach Pepper is hard as nails. He puts up with nothin' from nobody."

They finished their cones and pedaled back into the woods. When they reached Fivehead's driveway they stopped, side by side. "Thanks for the cone," Max said.

Fivehead took out his phone. "Give me your cell number, I'll give you mine." The boys swapped numbers, and Max pedaled toward his house. Rolling into his garage, he broke into a grin. *Fivehead's a crack-up. At least there's one cool kid on my team.*

CHAPTER 2

ENEMIES – ON HIS OWN TEAM

MAX WOKE THE NEXT MORNING to the rumble of a truck pulling into the driveway. He peeled back his shade. *The goals are here!* Glancing into his backyard, he saw his dad, mom, and sister, all on their knees, using prongs to dig out weeds.

Max pulled on a ratty pair of jeans, a tattered sweatshirt, and sneakers. He bounded down the stairs and out to the yard. "You're late, but not too late," Betsy said. She tossed her prong to him and pointed at a full wheelbarrow. "I dug up a hundred weeds, Max. You get the next hundred." Max knelt, jabbed the prong under a dandelion and flicked it out, roots and all.

By early afternoon, they had weeded the entire Square. Mr. Miles wheeled his lawn tractor out of the shed and set the blades on 'low.' Max hopped on and gave the lawn a fresh cut. After a lunch break, he helped his dad roll out one hundred and twenty yards of white chalk, thirty yards on each side. The border was set, the Square had taken shape.

After a rest, the whole family dragged a large goal onto the back line. On the other sides, they placed three smaller goals. As the sun began to set, Max and Betsy played keep-away from their mom. Mrs. Miles chased hard, but she couldn't get a foot on the ball. Finally, she threw up her hands. "You guys are too good, I surrender." As they walked off, Mr. Miles stepped onto the deck with a pitcher of water and glasses.

"What do you think, Max?"

"We made another Square, Dad, pretty cool."

After dinner that night, Max climbed the stairs and checked the underlined dates on his wall calendar.

Wednesday, September 2 – first Thunder practice
Saturday, September 5 – first game
Wednesday, September 9 – first day of school

First practice tomorrow, first game in four days. Max peered out his window. The sun had sunk low, the shadows from the trees stretching onto the Square. *Got enough daylight to get a few more touches on the ball.* He popped a text to Fivehead. *Come over, check out the Square.* The reply was fast: *On my way.* A few minutes later Max was juggling on the Square when Fivehead walked in. "Hey, I dig this Square!"

Max tapped to Fivehead. "Come on, let's rip a few." They fired balls at the big goal until darkness set in. When Max finished with four straight into the upper left corner, Fivehead shook his head. "How do you hit the corner like that?"

"Thirty minutes of shooting practice, every day."

Fivehead nodded. "Guess I should do the same thing."

After Fivehead left for home, Max went inside. His mom was in the kitchen. "I was watching you and Fivehead," she said. "You hit a few balls high."

"Come on, Mom, I'm not a machine."

Max went up and dropped on his bed. He stared at the ceiling – and saw Red Peters sneering back at him. He rolled over and buried his face in his pillow.

Dark clouds hung low as Max arrived at Liberty Park the next morning. Only Red Peters and Eddie Hazard were there, tapping a ball back and forth. Max hoped they would call him over, but they acted like he wasn't there. He sucked in a deep breath. *I can do this.* He jogged over. "Hey guys, can I join?"

Red glared at Max. "We're gonna run some laps." Red trotted off, Eddie close behind. Max flicked his ball up and began to juggle. *What's wrong with those guys?*

When every player had arrived, Coach Pepper called the team in. He walked up and rested a hand on Max's shoulder. "Boys, let's welcome the newest member of the Thunder, Max Miles." As Coach led the cheers, Max noticed that Red and Eddie clapped only twice. Coach peeled off his windbreaker. "Okay, time to stretch."

Fivehead swung his boot through the grass. "We're already loose, Coach."

Coach glared at Fivehead. "Wesley Cannon,

firing back at me again. Show us how fast you can do ten push-ups, boy."

"Sorry, Coach, I'm savin' my energy for practice."

"You're all energy, Wes," Coach shot back. "Now get down and get going."

Fivehead dropped, pumped out ten quick ones, and sprang up. "Okay, Coach, let's play."

Coach smirked at Fivehead. "Boys, think about a piece of bubble gum. When you put gum in, you can't blow a bubble right away, can you? You have to soften up the gum first. Think of your body the same way. You've got to loosen up your muscles before you can get the most out of them."

After Coach led the boys through some stretches, he pulled red and yellow T-shirts from his bag. He set up a scrimmage, Max and Red on opposing sides. As Max jogged out, he could feel his heart beat like a hammer under his shirt. *Back in Liverpool, everybody knew me. But now I'm the new kid, and being new stinks.*

Light rain wet the grass as play began. Max picked off a pass, fed Eddie on the flank, and broke for the box. Eddie crossed, but the keeper beat Max to the ball. "Come on, Max, that's your ball!" Eddie wailed. Max put up a hand, but wished he hadn't. *Give me time to get there, Eddie!*

His adrenaline pumping, Max swiped another pass and dribbled toward the goal. When a defender neared, Max saw Eddie running free to his right. He led Eddie into the box, but Eddie slowed and the keeper smothered the ball.

"Make the pass sooner!" Eddie yelped.

Max opened his mouth but swallowed his words. *These guys are idiots. No way I can play for this team.*

A bit later Max chased a loose ball on the flank, Red close behind. Max collected at full speed and pushed the ball down the line. As he tapped the ball again, Red slid and cut Max to the grass. "Aahh!" Max yelled. He held his left ankle, and Coach ran over. "You okay?" Coach asked. Max stood. Pain shot through his ankle. "I better take a break."

As Max hobbled to the bench, Coach called Red aside. Max turned his ear in their direction. "Red, that was a bad tackle," Coach snapped.

"You always tell me to tackle hard," Red volleyed.

"Tackle the ball, not your teammate's leg," Coach shot back.

Max smiled inside. *At least Coach is onto that kid.* Coach grabbed a bag of ice from his cooler and tossed it to Max. Max held it to his ankle and watched. When Red scored a bit later, Max tossed the bag aside and jogged up to Coach. "Coach, I'm ready."

"Sit for the rest of practice, Max."

"Coach, I gotta play."

Coach stared. "Let me see you run."

Max darted off five yards, turned and ran back. Coach waved him on. Max dashed out, ignoring the twinge he felt each time his left foot hit the ground. He ran onto a pass from Ben Kwan and dribbled into open space. He couldn't see Red, but he could feel him over his shoulder. Red slid, but this time, Max was ready. He pinched the ball between his boots and jumped. Red slid under Max, his cleats sticking up. As Red skimmed past, Max landed and dribbled to the edge of the box. A foe challenged, but Max cut around him and lashed his right instep into the ball.

The strike was pure. The ball whistled past the keeper and cracked the net in the far corner.

Coach blew his whistle. "Play on, boys. Red, come here!"

Red jogged over to Coach. "Go home, now," Coach snapped.

"I went in clean!" Red wailed.

"Bull, you went in studs up. If Max wasn't so quick, you would've taken him out. Call for a ride, now!"

Red fished out his phone and made the call. Then he picked up his bag and hurled it toward the lot. Max saw it all. *Fivehead was right, that kid is like a volcano going off.*

A bit later Coach called the team in. "Boys, time for our penalty kick contest. You miss once, you're out. Winner takes our PKs in games."

"But Red made all our PKs last year," Eddie whined. "He's not even here."

"Too bad for him," Coach retorted.

After seven rounds only two boys were still alive – Max and Eddie. As Max stepped up for his next shot, Eddie grabbed his arm. In a low voice he said, "Red should be takin' our PKs Max, you know it."

Max smiled inside. *Nice try, Eddie.* Max laced a low screamer that popped the net inches inside the post. Now it was do or die for Eddie. He cracked a hard shot, but it clanked the bar and bounced over. Eddie swung his boot through the grass. Coach called the boys in. "Max will take our penalty kicks."

"That's not fair," snapped Artie. "Max just joined the team, and he's gonna take the kicks?"

Coach fixed his eyes on Artie. "We had a contest, Artie. Max won. End of story."

Artie pressed on. "But Coach –"

"Can it, Artie," Coach hit back.

Coach swung his eyes to Max. "Max, I teach eighth-grade English at the middle school. I use words to help us focus. Today's word is 'UNSELFISH.' Anyone know what it means?"

Ben Kwan put up a hand. "It means putting other people before yourself."

"Bingo, Ben." Coach swung his eyes to Eddie. "I heard a lot of yapping today. That ends now, got it?"

The boys nodded, even Eddie. Coach walked over and put a hand on Max's shoulder. "Max, you're a great player, we're thrilled to have you."

Max smiled. Coach pulled the string tight on his ball bag. "Boys, we open the season against the Rockets on Saturday. We are one of ten teams in our league. We play each team once this fall. The top two teams qualify for the championship game in Philadelphia. Tell me, are we going to Philadelphia?"

"YES!" the boys shouted.

"Darn right," Coach snapped. "See you Tuesday."

As the boys walked off, Fivehead jogged up to Max. "Max, you were the best player on the field, even better than Red. Bet ya Coach makes you the center midfielder, moves Red outside."

"Who knows. I'm just glad I'm not playin' against Red. I mean, the guy is all cleats."

"Yeah, but like I said, Coach puts up with no bull."

"He sure smacked down Artie," Max said.

"Forget Fartie," Fivehead said. "He's all mouth, no muscle."

Max snorted at that.

At dinner that night, Betsy had big news. "I'm gonna start in goal on Saturday," she said.

"That's great, Bets!" Mr. Miles blared He looked at Max. "How about you, Max, good practice?"

Max stuck his fork into a pile of shepherd's pie. "Not so good. First, this Eddie kid kept yellin' at me. And then Red Peters slid into me, twice."

Betsy spiked her napkin. "That kid's crazy. You never take out a teammate."

"Coach kicked Red out of practice. Later, I won the penalty kick contest. Red took 'em last year."

"That's great, Max," his mom shot in. "You should take them, you're automatic."

Max stared out at the Square. *Wonder how Red will feel when I take the next penalty kick?*

He wouldn't have to wait long.

CHAPTER 3

RED IN THE FACE

S ATURDAY, GAME DAY. MAX SPRANG out of bed and hustled downstairs. His dad was making Max's usual pre-game breakfast – two strawberry pancakes, a sliced apple, and a piece of toast with peanut butter.

Max sat. Mr. Miles slid a full plate in front of him, along with a tall glass of apple juice. "You're going to have a big game, Max, I can feel it."

Max dribbled out a pool of syrup. "I've never had to worry about my own teammates. What if Red and Eddie bust on me during the game?"

"Coach Pepper will be all over it, I'm sure."

"I hope he has good ears," Max said.

An hour later, Mr. Miles swung his car into Liberty Park. As Max opened the door, Mrs.

Miles faced him. "Remember, Max, don't be afraid to shoot."

Without saying a word, Max got out and slammed the door shut. *I gotta deal with Red and Eddie, and now my mom pressures me to score. Unreal.* Max reached the field, dropped his bag by the bench, and stepped into a warm-up lap with Fivehead. As they got back to the bench, Max noticed Coach Pepper scribbling on his clipboard. *I wonder who's gonna be in the middle, me or Red?*

A few minutes later the Thunder huddled around Coach. Max could feel Red's eyes on him. Coach spoke. "We're making some changes at midfield. Max plays in the middle, Red on the left, Eddie on the right."

Red's mouth fell open. "But Coach, I play in the middle."

"Today you play on the left."

"But –"

"No more buts, Red, got it?"

Red curled his lips shut. Max glanced at Red, but when Red glared back, Max looked away. Coach put out a hand and the boys stacked theirs on top. "Let's take it to them from the start – show them we expect to win. Three, two, one, THUNDER!"

As Max took the field, he looked to the sidelines. He saw his dad, camera in hand. Mr. Miles stuck up a thumb, and Max nodded. Five minutes in, Max stole a back pass. Picking up speed toward the box, he had only one Rocket to beat. Red ran free to his left and called for the ball. But when the defender edged toward Red, Max cut left and lashed a bullet that flew just over the bar.

Red ran up. "I was wide open!"

"I had a good shot," Max fired back.

"I woulda scored!" Red wailed.

Max turned away, his heart pounding. Eddie jogged over. "Red was open, Max. And when Red's open, you give him the ball." Max said nothing, but inside, he burned.

Late in the first half, Fivehead cushioned a punt on his thigh and exploded down the flank. Max darted into an open seam and Fivehead played the ball into his path. Max ran on and unleashed from the eighteen. *Thwack!* He struck the ball so hard that nobody moved, not even the keeper. The shot rattled the far post and caromed into the net. Thunder 1, Rockets 0.

Max got mobbed by most of his teammates. But as he broke from the huddle, he saw that Red and Eddie were already back to their side. *I score, and those guys ignore me!*

Ten minutes later, a Rocket stole Artie's pass and surged toward the box. As Artie stepped up to challenge, Max broke into a sprint. The Rocket cut around Artie and entered the box alone. Thunder keeper Theo Swisher came out, but the boy weaved around him and took aim at the open goal. At the last second, Max lunged from the side. The shot hit his arm and flew out of bounds. The ref blew his whistle and pointed at the penalty spot.

Max hung his head. Red ran up. "You gave up a penalty kick, Max. Real smart."

Max felt his chest harden like a hunk of ice. Theo ran up. "Great hustle, Max, you almost saved me."

Max nodded at Theo. The Rocket put the ball on the spot. He stepped up and creamed a bolt into the corner. Thunder 1, Rockets 1. As Max jogged back, Eddie ran up. "Never again, Max."

Max bit his tongue. He glanced at his dad. Mr. Miles nodded, his hands open in front of his chest. Max nodded. *Forget about those idiots, just play your game.* A bit later, Max plucked the ball out of a forest of legs in the circle. Seeing Fivehead burst free down the flank, Max lofted the ball ahead of him. Fivehead gathered, dribbled into the box, and lashed a low dart that stung the net just inside the far post. Thunder 2, Rockets 1.

Fivehead ran over. "Great feed, Max!" Max looked toward his dad, who held up one finger. On the kickoff, the Rockets fed their speedy right wing. He blazed into the corner and struck a hard cross. Chipper Hines stepped up and smashed it out toward midfield. Max pumped his fists. *That should do it.* The Rocket left back ran up and thumped the bouncing ball, sending it high and far. Theo backpedaled and leaped, but the shot ducked inches under the bar. Thunder 2, Rockets 2.

Max met Fivehead in the circle. Red joined them. "I'll take off down the right side," Red said. "Get me the ball, I'll win this thing."

Fivehead tapped to Max. He sidestepped a hard-charging foe and floated a long ball down the right flank. Red collected on the run and juked past a defender into the box. He cut past a second foe, but the boy stuck out a late boot and took Red down hard. The ref blew his whistle and pointed at the spot – penalty kick for the Thunder.

Red gathered the ball and put it on the spot. "Max, you take it!" shouted Coach Pepper.

Red stared toward the bench. "I take the PKs."

"Max won the contest at practice, Red," Fivehead said.

"That's bull, I wasn't there!" Red shot back.

Max stepped toward the spot, but Red stuck a hand on his chest. "I got fouled, I'm takin' it."

Max felt a knot in his chest. "You heard Coach, it's my kick."

"Get out of the box, now," Red snapped.

Max turned away. Red lined up a few yards behind the ball. He stepped up and ripped a rocket. *Bonk!* The ball struck the bar and flew over. The Rocket keeper launched the goal kick, and the ref blew his final whistle. Thunder 2, Rockets 2.

As Max walked off, Artie ran up. "Max, that was your kick. You wimped out!"

Max blew out a long breath. *I already feel bad, and Artie has to pile on.*

As the boys reached the bench, Coach met

Red with an icy stare. "I said that was Max's kick, and I know you heard me."

Red kept his eyes on Coach's. "We crushed this team last year. Then you make all these changes, and we let them tie us. What do you say about that?"

Coach and Red went eye to eye for a few more beats. Then Coach turned to face the team. "My word for today is 'INCENSED.' It means really angry, and that's me right now. I'll see ya at practice. Except you, Red, you stick around."

Max wanted to hear that conversation. He was the last boy to collect his bag. As he stepped away, he glanced over his shoulder. Coach's chin was an inch from Red's nose. "You disobeyed me, Red Peters. I have a good mind to kick you off the team."

Max heard that, but he couldn't hear Red's response. When Max reached his family, his anger poured out. "Red butted in on my penalty kick!"

"That kid has some nerve," Mrs. Miles said as they got in the car. "What did Coach say after the game?"

"He balled out Red, but Red gave him lip right back."

"He's crazy!" Betsy cut in. "You never mouth off to a coach."

"Max, your goal was a stunner," Mr. Miles said.

"Yeah, but after I scored, Red and Eddie ignored me."

"They're a couple of punks," Mrs. Miles cut in. "I bet Coach Pepper would love to get rid of them."

"Maybe, but they score almost all the goals," Max said.

"That was before you joined the team," Mrs. Miles replied.

That night, Red and Eddie met in Red's treehouse. "So, Eddie, I got a new team. The Lightning."

Eddie's eyes bulged. "No way."

"Yep, Coach 'Pooper' gave me some lip after you guys left, so I told him I was gone. My dad called the coach of the Lightning. Turns out two kids quit their team last week. Their coach said he wants me."

Red picked up a rock and tossed it into the creek running behind the treehouse. "Eddie, in four weeks, the Lightning plays the Thunder. I can't wait, you and me, against our old team."

Eddie's eyebrows shot up. "What are ya sayin', Red?"

"The Lightning has one more opening, Eddie. You're comin' with me."

Eddie gulped. "Geez, Red, I don't know."

Red put his hands on Eddie's shoulders. "Look, me and you led the league in scoring last year, forty-seven goals between us. We gotta stick together. I know it, you know it."

Eddie felt Red's fiery eyes burning through him. "You're right, Red. I'm in."

Red held up his palm, and Eddie slapped it. A grin slid across Red's face. "I can't wait 'til we play the Thunder. Ya know, Eddie, lightning always comes before thunder. It's true in the sky. It's true in the dictionary. And it's gonna be true in the standings."

CHAPTER 4
FROM THUNDER TO LIGHTNING

A S MAX DID HIS STRETCHES before practice on Monday, he noticed that Red and Eddie weren't there. *That's weird, they're always here first*. Minutes later Coach Pepper blew his whistle, and the boys gathered around. Before Coach could speak, Artie asked the question on every boy's mind. "Where's Red and Eddie?"

Coach blew out a sigh. "They quit the team," he said. "Red quit after the game Saturday, and then Eddie sent me a note yesterday."

Max's jaw fell open. Chatter shot through the huddle, until Coach put up a hand. "Red and Eddie were lousy teammates," he said. "They were so unfair to Max. And then Red takes that penalty kick, against my direction. That about sent me to the moon."

"I'm glad they're gone," Fivehead snapped. "They join another team?"

"Yep, the Lightning," Coach said.

"Good," Fivehead answered. "We play them in a few weeks, we'll crush 'em."

Max felt his pulse jump. *Wonder what's worse, playing with Red, or against him?*

Artie looked at Coach. "Red and Eddie scored almost all of our goals."

"We have plenty of scorers," Coach lobbed back. "Plus, I know Max will score a bunch."

Max twisted his cleats in the grass. *Score a bunch?*

"But what about our lineup?" Artie asked.

"Louie and Scooter will flank Max at midfield," Coach said.

Coach set up a scrimmage. Max took the field. *No Red, no Eddie. I don't have to worry about getting balled out, or chopped to the ground.* For the next hour, Max felt like he had been set free. He ran hard, but never felt winded. He scored three goals, and set up two more. After Max lashed in his last goal, Coach called the boys in. "Max, come here," Coach called out.

Max stepped up, and Coach put a hand on his shoulder. "You know why Max is always around the ball?" Coach asked, and then he answered his own question. "Because he's 'ASSERTIVE.' Anyone know what that means?"

The boys looked at Ben, but he put up his hands. Coach went on. "Assertive means 'confident and determined.' When a teammate gets the ball, Max doesn't watch, he moves. He asserts himself." Coach paced, but he wasn't done. "Great players *want* the ball. They go to it. They don't wait for it to come to them."

A bit later, Coach ended practice. As Max went for his bag, he felt a thorn jabbing him. *Red left because of me, so did Eddie.* That wasn't the only thorn. *Coach said I'll score a bunch. First my mom, now Coach.*

While the other boys headed to the lot, Max paced near the bench. Coach was filling his ball bag when he noticed him. "What's up, Max?"

Max stared into the grass. "Coach, I'm sorry."

Coach cocked his head sideways. "Sorry for what?"

"I messed up the team. Red and Eddie left because of me."

Coach rested a hand on Max's shoulder. "Look, if Red hadn't quit, I was gonna boot him off the team. Truth is, I'd rather have you than Red and Eddie. I mean, you're the best player I've ever coached. But you know what I like most about you? You're a big player, but you don't have a big head."

Max scratched his cleats in the grass. "Coach, I'm not *that* good. You say I'll score a lot of goals. That's pressure."

"Max, just do your best, that's all I ask."

"Sounds good, Coach."

Coach pointed at the parking lot. "You better get goin', before your dad falls asleep."

Max hustled over and got in the car. "Dad, you won't believe it. Red quit the team, so did Eddie."

"Wow, Max, how do you feel?"

"I felt great at first, then kinda guilty. But Coach said it wasn't my fault."

"Coach is right," Mr. Miles said. "Those guys were all about themselves."

Max went on. "I think Coach expects me to score a lot. Now if I don't score, people will think I had a bad game."

"Look, Max, no one scores in every game," Mr. Miles said. "The best strikers in the world, they don't score in half their games. They focus on winning, not scoring."

Max smiled inside. *Dad's cool, no pressure.*

When Max got home, he got out his notebook and jotted down Coach's latest word. Assertive – confident and determined. He looked at the other words on his list. Unselfish. Incensed. *Wow, Coach sure knows a bunch of big words. He must have a big brain.*

That afternoon, Max, Betsy and their mom shopped for school supplies. As Max picked out notebooks it hit him – he actually wanted school to start. *Since I moved, soccer's been everything. I'm ready for something besides soccer.* Before long they had snaked through every aisle, stuffing the cart with notebooks, rulers, pens, hi-liters, and wall calendars. As they stood in line to pay, Mrs. Miles put up a hand. "Be right back," she said, jogging off. A minute later she came back and flipped a notepad into the cart.

"What's that for?" Max asked.

"So I can take notes at your games."

Max looked at Betsy. She threw up her hands, as if to say, *Why bother to argue?* Max let out a long breath. *Why can't Mom be more chill, like Dad?*

That night, Max was loading up his backpack when his phone dinged. It was an email from Red. *Nice going, Miles. You move to Chelsea and break up the Thunder. You know who the best team is now? That's right, the Lightning. In a few weeks we're gonna crush the Thunder, and you're gonna feel like the biggest loser in the world.*

His heart racing, Max fired his phone into his pillow. *That kid really creeps me out.*

Wednesday, the first day of sixth grade. Max's alarm was set for 6:30, but he woke at 6:08. As he stepped into his faded blue jeans, he thought about the alphabet. *My last name starts with M, Red's starts with P. He probably won't be in my homeroom, but with my luck, he'll be in all my classes.*

Max poured a big bowl of cereal, but ate only a few bites. Then he and Betsy stepped out into a steady rain. When Max reached the sidewalk, he spied Fivehead and jogged to catch up. "Rain's comin' down hard," Max said.

Fivehead nodded. "This rain will fill the creek behind our yards. Great day to race sticks."

"Race sticks?" Max echoed.

"Show ya after school," Fivehead said. The bus pulled up, and the boys got on and sat in the back. Fivehead got out his phone and opened his ESPN app, and the boys watched highlights from the English Premier League games played that weekend. When they reached the school, Max could feel his pulse race. His homeroom was on one side, Fivehead's on the other. At the first intersection of halls, they went separate ways. Suddenly, Max felt alone, and invisible. *Back in Liverpool, everyone knew me. Here, I'm like a ghost.*

Max got to his homeroom and sat in the front row. When the bell rang, he looked around, no Red. After three classes, Max's luck had held up. At lunch he bought a chocolate milk and found teammates Fivehead, Ben, Theo, and Chipper at a table. As Max bit into his baloney sandwich, he spotted Red and Eddie across the room. *The farther away, the better.*

After lunch, Max's lucky streak kept going. Seven classes – no Red, and no Eddie either. Only one class to go – social studies. Max checked his map and found his way to the classroom. He sat in the front row and glanced around. *No Red, this is awesome.*

The bell rang, and Mrs. Dingle rose from behind her desk. Suddenly the door swung open. Max looked back, and in walked Red. He sat in the back row, next to Ben Kwan. Mrs. Dingle took off her glasses and tucked her straight blond hair behind her ears. She eyed Red. "Students, I expect everyone to be in their seats *before* the bell rings." Max fought off a smile. *Red makes enemies wherever he goes.*

A minute later, Mrs. Dingle turned to write on the blackboard. That's when Max felt something hit the back of his head. He reached up and plucked a spitball out of his hair. A few students giggled. Mrs. Dingle turned around. "What's going on?" she asked.

Ben started to speak, but Red kicked his foot. Mrs. Dingle swung her eyes from face to face. Max stared straight ahead. Finally, Mrs. Dingle crossed her arms. "I'm warning you now, kids, I won't put up with any more shenanigans."

When class ended, Mrs. Dingle asked Max to stay. Once the other students had left, she sat next to him. "Max, when I asked what was going on, I could see something in your expression."

"Someone hit me with a spitball, no big deal."

"I bet I know who it was," Mrs. Dingle said. "I've got my eye on him."

"Sounds good, Missus Dingle."

Max stood and walked out. *I had a shutout going until my last class, and then Red shows up. Kinda like giving up a tie-breaking goal in the last minute.*

A bit later, Max headed for the bus. He got on and found Fivehead in back. "Good day?" Fivehead asked.

"Until last period," Max said. "Red's in my social studies class."

"Don't sweat it, Max. I give him one week before he gets thrown out of school."

Max snorted. "So Fiver, tell me about racing sticks."

"We pick sticks out of the woods," Fivehead explained. "We put 'em in the creek where it bends behind your house. We follow the sticks along. If your stick gets stuck, you can set it free. The finish line is the footbridge behind my house. First stick under it wins."

"Sounds cool, Fiver."

Twenty minutes later the boys met in Max's backyard. Max followed Fivehead as he traipsed through low bushes leading to the creek. When they reached the water, Fivehead smiled. "Creek's at least six inches deep, our sticks are gonna cruise." The boys poked in the leaves until each had found a stick. "Okay, we gotta name our sticks," Fivehead said. "Mine's 'Blitz.'" Max thought. "Mine's 'Torpedo.'" Fivehead nodded. "Good one, for a rookie."

They bent and held their sticks over the water. "One, two, three go!" Fivehead called. Max's stick raced ahead, but then it ran up on a rock. Max reached in and freed it, but Blitz was now six feet ahead. The boys trotted along as their sticks floated down the creek. Twenty feet from the bridge, Torpedo had pulled even. But Blitz surged at the end, and won by half-a-stick.

Fivehead looked at Max. "Sorry, dude, I never lose." Max laughed. "Next time, I'll get revenge."

At dinner that night, Betsy shared some news. "So Max, guess who my English teacher is?"

"Gotta be Coach Pepper."

"Yep, he's so cool. And he thinks you're awesome."

Max nodded. *Yeah, and he expects a lot of me.* Mr. Miles spooned a pile of Spanish rice onto Max's plate. "So Max, how was school?"

"Okay, until my last class. My biggest fan is in it."

"Let me guess, Red Peters," Mrs. Miles said, and Max nodded. "He hit me in the head with a spitball."

"At least he's off your soccer team," Betsy said.

"Yeah, and now I gotta get him off my back."

CHAPTER 5

RIDING A BICYCLE – UPSIDE DOWN

AX WOKE ON SATURDAY, HIS eyes on the black uniform spread on his carpet. *Thunder has no color, but if it did, I guess it would be black.* Max sprang up and put on his shirt, shorts, and socks. He smiled in the mirror. *Red and Eddie are gone, time to tear it up.*

From the opening whistle, Max ran like a deer. Five minutes in he swiped a pass, cut around two foes, and eyed the frame from twenty yards. *Keeper's out, he's gonna pay.* Max stubbed his boot under the ball. It arced up. The keeper backpedaled and leaped. The ball flew over his hands, kissed the bottom of the bar, and dropped in the net. Max got mobbed by his teammates, all of them this time.

Five minutes later, Max stripped the ball from

the center back and charged into the box alone. The keeper ran out. Max faked a shot, dropping the keeper into a slide. Then he cut around him and lashed a bolt into the open net. Max turned and started to run, but Fivehead tackled him. "Dude, you're movin' like a torpedo!" Fivehead cracked.

Late in the game, Fivehead dribbled free down the flank and thumped a hard cross to the back post. Max ran on, soared over a defender, and snapped into a header. The ball bounced under the keeper's hands and punched the net. In the last minute, Max beat three guys off the dribble and stepped into a thunderous drive. The ball knuckled over the keeper's hands and rang the bar. The rebound fell to Fivehead, and he calmly tucked it into a corner. Thunder 4, Eagles 0.

After the final whistle, the boys huddled around Coach Pepper. He looked at Max. "Max, you got Thunder in your boots, boy."

"Max, Max, Max!" the boys chanted. Coach went on. "My word for the day is, 'CONCENTRATION'. It means intense focus. We lost two players this week, but you stayed locked in on your game. Great work, see you next week."

Max grabbed his bag and trotted over to his family. "I've never seen you play better, Max," Mr. Miles raved.

"That was some header, Max," Betsy added. "You were like, three feet off the ground."

Max laughed. "Maybe two feet, Bets."

Mrs. Miles was next. "Three goals, Max, that puts a smile on my face."

Max smirked. "Don't expect a hat trick every game, Mom."

The next morning Max hustled down for the paper, but Betsy had beaten him to it. He found her at the kitchen table, *The Chelsea Chimes* newspaper open in front of her. Betsy finished reading and slid the paper to Max. "You're gonna like this story, Max."

Max read the headline first.

MILES POWERS THUNDER OVER EAGLES

Then he read the story. *Newcomer Max Miles rang up three goals and an assist to lead the Thunder to a 4-0 romp over the Eagles in u-12 soccer action. Five minutes in, Miles beat two players off the dribble and chipped a rainbow over the keeper and under the bar. Later in the half Miles broke in alone, swerved around the keeper, and drilled into the empty cage. Miles completed his hat trick in the second half when he leaped over a defender and nodded a powerful header past the keeper. "Max is a dynamic player," said Thunder Coach Jack Pepper. "When he gets the ball, you expect something special to happen." In the closing minutes, Miles lashed a thunderous drive off the bar, and teammate Wesley Cannon tucked home the rebound. Miles joined the Thunder this summer after moving from Liverpool, New Jersey. He and Cannon give the Thunder a potent strike force. "Max is a magician," Cannon said. "He does things with the ball we've never seen before."*

Max pumped a fist. *Wish I could see Red's face when he reads this.* Max eyed the league standings next to the article. With one win and one tie, the Thunder sat tied for third place. *Plenty of time to make up ground – and get to Philadelphia.*

Max was peeling a banana when Fivehead called. "Max, you see the paper?"

"Yeah, your quote's kind of embarrassing."

"Get outta here, it's true."

As Max finished up with Fivehead, Mrs. Miles walked in. She read the story. "Max, this is some article. A magician, huh? I love it."

"Yeah, Mom, but bet I get needled tomorrow."

Max was right. On his way to homeroom on Monday, he saw Red coming his way. Max lowered his head and angled across the hall, but Red slid into his path. "Scored three goals, huh, Miles?" Red snapped. "Big deal, I scored four. Told ya, Miles, I win the scoring title, Lightning wins the league. You got that, punk?"

Max tried to step around, but Red shuffled in front of him. "I can't wait to play you in three weeks, Miles. I'm gonna run you over, make it the worst day of your life."

Red stormed off, leaving Max frozen like a statue. *That kid creeps me out. Why can't I stand up to him?*

After lunch, Max was nearing his locker when he felt a large hand drop on his shoulder. He turned to find Coach Pepper smiling down at him. "Come with me, Max, I got an offer you can't refuse." Max trailed Coach Pepper through a hallway packed with students. Coach cut an easy path to follow. Standing six-foot-three with shoulders as wide as a door, Coach always had an open lane ahead of him. When they reached Coach's room, Coach sat at his desk and Max sat opposite. Coach opened a drawer, pulled out an envelope, and tossed it to Max. It slipped through Max's hands and landed in his lap. "You're no keeper, are ya?" Coach quipped. "Open it."

Max took out three tickets. Coach smiled. "You're holding tickets to tonight's Philadelphia Kicks game. That's the new pro team. I wanna take you and your sister. It's my way of welcoming you to Franklin Middle School."

"That's awesome!" Max gushed. "I've never been to a pro game."

As the day wore on, Max's mind wandered ahead to the Kicks' game. In social studies class, Mrs. Dingle asked him to name the capital of Tennessee, but he didn't answer. She got up and walked over to him. "Earth to Max Miles, anybody home?"

The class roared. "Sorry, Missus Dingle. I was thinking about something else."

"Soccer, I'll bet. Let's try again. What's the capital of Tennessee?"

"Knoxville?"

"You got the second half right. It's Nashville."

As his classmates snickered, Max felt his face go flush. Later, Mrs. Dingle grabbed a stick of chalk and scribbled on the board. *First term project: write a three-hundred-word paper on a "global trend that affected the world."*

Riding the bus home, Max thought about the assignment. *"A global trend that affected the world?"* He shook his head. *What a snooze.* Max was the last one off the bus. He jogged twenty yards to catch up with Betsy on the sidewalk. "Coach invited us to the Kicks game tonight."

"I know, he asked me after class," Betsy said. "Hope Mom lets us go."

"Me too," Max said. "Beat ya home."

Max took off, Betsy hot on his trail. Betsy edged ahead, but Max hopped over the hedge, bolted across the lawn, and beat her to the porch by one stride. Inside they found their mom at the computer in her den, working on her novel. "Mom, Coach Pepper invited us to the Kicks game tonight," Max said, catching his breath. "Can we go, please?"

Mrs. Miles took off her glasses. "Get your homework done, and you can go."

Max held up a palm, and Betsy slapped it.

Three hours later Coach Pepper, Max, and Betsy reached the parking lot at the Kicks' stadium. As Coach eased his red pick-up into a spot, a soccer ball thumped his windshield. "Whoa!" Max yelled. Coach laughed. "Don't sweat it, Max. I just drove my pick-up into a pick-up game."

Max looked around. Soccer balls flew all over. He saw a boy trip over a ball and skin his knee on the pavement. The boy popped up and chased the ball, unaware of the blood trickling down his shin. Max breathed in the aroma of hot dogs, hamburgers, and sausages rising off grills. "Coach, this is like a huge party," he observed.

Coach took his grill out of the back and set it up. "It is a huge party, Max. Some fans have so much fun tailgating, they don't even go to the game."

"Why's it called 'tailgating?'" Betsy asked.

Coach swept his arms out. "Look at the

cars. People serve food and drinks from their tailgates."

A ball rolled toward Max. He flicked it up, pushed it higher with his thigh, headed it, and then caught it on top of his foot. A boy jogged up. "Man, you juggle good," the boy said. Max eyed the big blue 'K's painted on the boy's cheeks. "Nice paint job," Max said as he tapped the ball back.

When the grill got hot, Coach unpacked three sausage links, green peppers, and onions. While Coach cooked, Max and Betsy jumped into a game. A bit later, Max tore into a sausage sub. "Coach, you're an awesome cook."

Coach smiled. "And you thought all I can do is teach English and coach soccer, huh, kid?"

After they ate, Coach led the way into the stadium. They went up an escalator and down to their seats, just five rows from the field. "Awesome seats!" Max blared.

"We can see everything from here," Coach said. "The expressions on the players' faces, even the sweat on their foreheads. You never see that on TV."

Early in the game, a Kicks wing curled a cross into the box, slightly behind the striker.

The striker slowed and turned his back to the goal. As the ball neared, he leaped, leaned back, swung one leg up and then whipped his other leg at the ball. As the ball flew off his boot, he crashed to the ground. The acrobatic kick froze the keeper like a monument. The ball sailed clean into the far corner. "What a shot!" Max yelled. "How'd he do that?"

"It's called a bicycle kick," Coach said. "Your legs move like they do when you ride a bike. It's also called an overhead kick."

Max watched the replay on the scoreboard. *That kick is cool, I gotta learn how to do it.*

At halftime, Max and Betsy followed Coach to the concession stand. Coach dug out a twenty-dollar bill and gave it to Betsy. "Get some drinks and peanuts, I'll be right back." As Coach trotted off, Betsy turned to Max. "Did Coach say what kind of drink he wants?"

"The cooler under his desk is wall-to-wall root beer," Max said. "He guzzles like, six cans a day. Fivehead calls him, 'Coach Boot Rear.'"

"Fivehead's quite the comic," Betsy said. "I'm sure Coach is tempted to boot him in the rear."

Max chuckled. He was about to order when

he felt a shove in the back. "Move it, Miles, no wimps allowed in this line."

Max turned to find Red Peters, in his face again. Max fumbled for words, but Betsy didn't. "Back off, Red. You wish you could play like Max."

Red glared at Betsy, noticed her keeper's shirt. "You play keeper, huh? I could score on you from midfield."

"You couldn't beat her on a penalty kick," Max snapped.

Red grabbed a plastic bottle of mustard and aimed it at Max's chest. But then Coach Pepper's heavy hand landed on his shoulder. "Red Peters, got a hot dog to go with that mustard?"

Red tossed the bottle aside and stormed off. Coach eyed Max. "You okay?"

"Yeah," Max muttered.

Coach stepped up to the counter and bought a root beer, two sports drinks, and a large bag of peanuts. "Let's go, the second half is starting."

When they got back to their seats, Betsy turned to Max. "Red Peters is a punk with a capital 'P' "

"Just my luck, I run into him here," Max whined.

"He made you shrink, Max. You gotta stand up to him."

"I'm trying."

"Try harder. You play against him soon, right? You gotta beat him like a dirty rug. That'll shut him up for good."

Max nodded, but said nothing.

The Kicks won, 2-0. When Coach pulled up at the Miles' house an hour later, Max was itching to get out a ball. "Watch me try one bicycle kick, Bets," he said as he fetched a ball from the garage.

"It's dark, Max."

"We can put on the spotlight. Come on, just one."

Betsy sighed. "Hurry up." She flicked on the light and followed Max out to the Square. He lobbed the ball up. As it started down, Max jumped and leaned back. He whipped his left foot up and swung his right foot at the ball. The ball hit his shin, popped up, and landed on his chin. Max jumped up. "Harder than it looks."

"Yeah, especially in the dark," Betsy said. "Come on, let's go in."

"One more, I'll jump sooner."

This time Max got his boot on the ball,

sending a weak roller across the lawn. "Better," Betsy said. "Let's go."

Max collected the ball. *I'm gonna learn that kick, no matter how much work it takes.*

CHAPTER 6

MAX VERSUS THE COBRAS:
WHO GET SQUEEZED?

T HE COACH OF THE COBRAS had read the *Chelsea Chimes*. He knew about Max, and he had a plan to stop him.

From the start, two Cobras coiled around Max. He ran hard to get open, but he couldn't escape the snake pit. When the Thunder got a goal kick, Coach Pepper called over Max, Ben, and Fivehead. "I want Max to work the left flank," Coach said. "Wesley and Ben, you should have room down the right. Get to the corner and launch crosses. Max will be on the prowl from the other side."

Fivehead and Ben ruled the right side and launched a string of hopeful crosses. But the Cheetah keeper bolted off his line and snagged every ball. As halftime neared, Ben hit a deep cross. Max blew past the two foes in his shadow and jumped, but all he headed was air. As Max tumbled to the grass, he saw the keeper come down with the ball. Max slapped the dirt. *That kid is a vacuum. I haven't sniffed the goal.*

In the stands, Mrs. Miles looked at Betsy. "Max has hardly touched the ball."

"He's got two or three guys on him, Mom. His teammates need to make the Cobras pay."

Just before the half, the Thunder earned a free kick on the flank. Max ran to Fivehead and whispered, "Far post." Fivehead floated the kick high and deep. As Max ran toward the ball, he saw the keeper barreling toward him. Max leaped and stuck out his head. This time, he got his head on something, but it wasn't the ball. It was the keeper's fist. Max tipped over like a sack of potatoes.

The keeper had punched away the cross, just before Max got his head to it. The keeper's fist followed through into Max's eye. Max felt like he had run into an oak tree. He scrambled up and took a few wobbly steps. Fivehead and Ben helped him to the bench. Coach gave him an icepack to put on his eye.

At halftime, the score was nil-nil. The Cobras had crossed the center line only twice. They seemed willing to settle for a scoreless draw. Coach Pepper walked over and sized up Max's eye. "You've got the beginnings of a nasty black eye, Max. You're finished today."

Max slammed his ice pack into the grass. "I'm goin' back in!" he yelled.

Coach eyed him, and Max put up his hands. "Sorry, didn't mean to shout. But Coach, my eye doesn't hurt. You gotta let me play."

"Max, Max, Max!" chanted his teammates. Artie even joined in. Coach Pepper could see the fire in Max's eyes. "I'll put you back in, but I've got an eye on you. If you look off, you're back on the bench."

"Coach, we got a problem," Fivehead said. "Their keeper is like my little brother, he eats everything. What do we do?"

Coach bit back a smile. "Most of your crosses are too close to goal," he said. "Don't give the keeper easy fruit to pick. Hit your crosses hard and low, and keep them twelve yards off his line."

The Thunder followed Coach's advice but the Cobra keeper picked all the fruit, ranging far off his line to haul in every cross. The Thunder's best chance came when Max swiped a pass and sprang Ben free, but Ben's low drive was gobbled by the keeper. When the keeper's punt landed out of bounds near midfield, Max looked toward his dad. Mr. Miles lifted his foot up and tapped it. Max smiled. *Great idea!* As Fivehead picked up the ball, Max dropped to a knee. "Dang, pebble in my cleat."

Max pulled off his left boot and banged the heel on the ground. Fivehead threw the ball in front of Ben down the flank. The two Cobras marking Max watched Ben race for the ball. Max tossed his boot aside and bolted for goal. Over his shoulder, he saw both Cobras ten yards behind.

As Max neared the box, Ben rolled a low ball into his path. Short a boot, Max knew he had only one chance. Nearing the ball in the arc, he slowed and swung his right boot into it. The Cobra keeper dove and got fingers on the ball. It bounced once, nicked the inside of the post, and trickled over the line.

Max ran at Ben. They bumped chests and fell to the grass. Fivehead piled on. "Max, you faked those guys out of their boots!"

Max snorted. "Better go get my other one." He jogged back up the field. His boot wasn't there. He looked to the bench. "You see my boot?" Coach put up his hands. Max looked at the Cobras' bench. *Bet they took it.*

Max played the last minute on one boot. The Thunder hung on to win, 1-0. Max jogged to the bench, and Coach Pepper wrapped an arm around him. "Great work, but your eye is swelling up," Coach said. He jogged to his cooler, dug out another icepack, and tossed it to Max.

The Thunder players shook hands with the Cobras. As Ben reached the end of the line, he spotted Max's shoe under the Cobras' bench. He picked it up and gave it to Max. The boys gathered around Coach. He took off his cap and shook his head. "Did you guys see what Max did before he scored?"

"It was crazy," Fivehead broke in. "He pretends he's got a stone in his shoe. The two guys marking him look away. Max gets up and springs free. He left his boot behind – and he left those goofballs in the rear view mirror."

Coach broke into a smile. "Thirty years

coaching soccer, and I've never seen that. Only you, Max."

"I did it once a few years ago," Max said. "When Fivehead got the throw-in, I looked at my dad. He tapped his shoe, and that's what gave me the idea."

"Your dad gets an assist on that goal," Fivehead cracked.

Coach spoke. "My word for the day is 'WILY.' It means 'skilled at gaining an advantage.'"

But then Artie threw a wet blanket on the celebration. "Why do the scorers always get all the credit?" Artie griped. "I mean, we shut that team out."

The huddle fell silent. Coach eyed Artie. "Artie, you and the back line played great. Keep it up."

Max looked at Artie. *That kid is a whiny brat.*

Coach put up a hand. "Boys, we have a huge game coming up next Saturday. We play the only team in the league with a perfect record, the Lightning. You'll be playing against two of your old teammates – Red Peters and Eddie Hazard."

Fivehead jabbed his right fist into his left

palm. "We're gonna crush those punks!" The boys roared.

After dinner that night, Max opened his computer and checked the league standings.

Team	Wins (3)	Losses (0)	Ties (1)	Pts
Lightning	3	0	0	9
Hornets	2	0	1	7
Thunder	2	0	1	7
Flash	2	0	1	7
Cobras	1	1	1	4
Eagles	1	2	0	3
Rampage	1	2	0	3
Torpedoes	0	2	1	1
Dragons	0	2	1	1
Volcanoes	0	3	0	0

Next, Max clicked on 'Leading Scorers.'

Player	Team	Goals	Assists	Pts
Miles	Thunder	5	2	12
Peters	Lightning	5	1	11
Stoneman	Hornets	4	3	11
Hazard	Lightning	3	3	9

Max smiled. *I lead the league in scoring, at least Mom will be happy about that.*

All week, Max tried not to think about Thunder versus Lightning. But then he saw Red walk into social studies class on Friday. *I want to beat that punk so bad.* At the start of class, Mrs. Dingle stepped in front of her desk with a hat in her hand. "It's time for your first team project," she said. "I've put your names in this hat. I'll pull two names at a time, and those will be our teams."

Max quickly counted up the students, twenty. *There's no way I get paired with Red.* Mrs. Dingle went through eight pairs without calling Max or Red. Only four names were left. She pulled out two more slips. "Tommy and Caroline," she said. Max felt a shiver dance on his spine. *That leaves only me and Red.*

Mrs. Dingle spent the rest of class meeting with each team. When she got to Max and Red, both boys looked like they had been locked in jail. "Okay boys, you both play soccer, so you know about the importance of walls," Mrs. Dingle said. "I want you to do a report on two famous walls – any kind of walls. I want you to compare your walls to someone you know –

and tell the class why each wall reminds you of that person."

Red looked at Mrs. Dingle. "Max said he doesn't want to be my partner."

"That's a lie!" Max blurted.

"That's enough!" Mrs. Dingle cut in. "Now get to work."

Both boys got out their phones and started searching for famous walls. Red found one first. "Okay, Miles, I'm doing the Great Wall in China."

"But – "

"Find your own wall, boy. I saw one in Israel, it's called the Wailing Wall. Sounds perfect for you, you little baby."

Red went back to his seat. For the next five minutes, Max watched the clock. At the sound of the bell, he hustled for the door. When he stepped into the hall, Red swooped in. "You're dead meat tomorrow, Miles," Red warned. "You wrecked the Thunder. And tomorrow you're gonna pay, big time."

Max opened his mouth but nothing came out. Red turned away, and Max hung his head. *Will I ever stand up to that kid?* Max walked to his locker and put away his books. On his way to the bus, he saw Eddie Hazard walking toward him. "Hey Eddie," Max said. Eddie slowed and glared. "If you're smart, you won't even show up tomorrow, Miles." Eddie walked away. Max felt his heart pound.

Max reached the bus and joined Fivehead in the back seat. "This day lasted a month," Fivehead cracked. "I am so psyched for tomorrow."

"Me too," Max murmured. Fivehead nudged his shoulder. "You sound like a mouse."

"Red just jumped me in the hall," Max said. "Bet he tries to take me out tomorrow."

"Look, Max, we win tomorrow, I bet Red never bothers you again."

"Hope you're right, Fiver."

When Max got home, he flipped his backpack on his desk. He stood on his bed, jumped, and whipped his right leg over his head. "*Boing*" went the springs as Max landed and bounced a foot in the air. He practiced a bicycle kick three more times. When he landed the last time, he heard his bed frame crack.

"What's that noise, Max?" Mrs. Miles called from down the hall.

"Nothin', Mom." *Guess I better find another place to practice my bicycle kick.*

In bed that night, Max kept seeing Red's face. He felt the sting in his eyes, heard the hate in his voice. Max gritted his teeth. *No more wimping out, Max. Tomorrow, you gotta fight back.*

CHAPTER 7

SHOWDOWN: THUNDER MEETS LIGHTNING

N SATURDAY, MAX WOKE TO noises in his belly. He rolled over but the sounds kept coming. *It's like the fourth of July in my stomach, fireworks going off.* Max flopped this way and that way, but he couldn't find a groove. Finally, he threw back his covers and went down to the kitchen, where his dad was pouring pancake batter into a frying pan.

"Not hungry, Dad."

"You need to eat, Max."

"I feel like I just ate a whole pizza."

"You thinking about Red Peters?"

Max nodded. "What if he goes after me, like he did in practice?"

"Give it right back, Max. Go hard for the

ball, within the rules. When Red realizes he can't intimidate you, he'll back off, you watch."

Mr. Miles peeled a banana and put it in front of Max. "Eat that, at least."

Max forced it down.

Two hours later the Miles' reached the field. Max got out and looked up at swollen gray clouds sweeping in. As he jogged for the Thunder bench, a strong gust shook leaves off the trees. A bit later, Max and Fivehead shared warm-up passes in their half of the circle. Fivehead struck a stray ball that flew over Max and into the Lightning's end. Red saw it. He stepped up and blasted the ball deep into the Thunder's half. "Get off our side!" Red snapped. Max jogged after the ball. *What an idiot!*

Coach Pepper called in the Thunder. He took a few seconds to lock eyes with each boy. When Coach looked at Max, Max noticed a vein popping out of his neck. *Wow, I've never seen Coach this fired up.* Coach put out his hand, and the boys stacked theirs on top. "It's game on, boys, let me hear ya. Three, two, one, THUNDER!"

The Thunder seized an early edge when Ben gathered a loose ball and led Fivehead to the corner. Max took off for the box, his eyes on Fivehead's cross. The ball curled in behind Max, and he knew it was time. *Bicycle kick.*

Max slowed, turned his back to goal, and leaped. Leaning back, he swung his left leg up and whipped his right boot at the ball. Max whiffed, his back thumping hard on the turf. A Lightning defender blasted the ball across midfield. Red jogged up to Max. "That was hilarious, Miles. You're such a doofus."

In the stands, Max's mom bowed her head. "That was painful to watch."

Betsy glared at her. "When was the last time you tried a bicycle kick, Mom?"

Max was eager to put his miscue behind him. He stripped the ball from Eddie and spun into the circle, but Red was waiting. Red made a clean tackle and Max kissed the dirt.

"Let's go, Eddie!" Red yelled as he pushed the ball ahead. Ben charged at him, but Red dinked to Eddie and Eddie tapped back into Red's path. Red dribbled once into the arc and unloaded. Theo dove, but the ball sizzled past his hands and rattled the cords. Lightning 1, Thunder 0.

Red dashed up the sideline, waving his

arms. Passing the Thunder bench, he pointed a finger at Coach Pepper. On the field, Max felt a tap on the shoulder. "You can't beat Red off the dribble, Max," Artie sniped. "You cost us a goal." Max looked away. *For once, Artie's right. That was my fault, I have to even the score.*

Max ran hard for the rest of the half, but Red and Eddie built a fence around him. A few times Max shook free and ran onto passes, but each time Red and Eddie quickly bottled him up. When Max reached the bench at halftime, Coach called him aside. "Max, you look tired. Wanna sit for a bit?"

"No way, Coach, I'll play better."

As Max jogged out for the second half, he looked over at his dad. Mr. Miles pumped his fists, and Max nodded back. When the whistle blew, Max found his gait. Taking a pass from Ben, he darted away from Red and dribbled into open grass. When Eddie stepped up, Max scissored over the ball. Eddie wobbled like a slow-rolling frisbee, and Max blew past.

As Max neared the edge of the box, he could feel Red closing fast. Max cocked his leg as if to shoot, drawing Red into a slide. Then Max cut the ball behind his planted leg, and Red tackled air. Max glanced up and saw a window. *Boom!* He cracked a bullet that froze the keeper and lashed the net in the far corner. Thunder 1, Lightning 1.

As his teammates swarmed on him, Max had a message. "Ties are for wimps, guys. Let's win this thing!"

Now Max's fuse was lit, and he began to take over. He beat Red and Eddie to fifty-fifty balls, set up good chances with precise feeds to the front line, and even jiggled the bar on a smash from twenty yards. In the stands, Mrs. Miles cracked a smile. "Max is all over the place."

Betsy nodded. "He's gonna win this thing, you watch."

But Red had other ideas. When the ball rolled out of play, he called Eddie over. "Miles is their only threat, we gotta get rid of him."

Eddie nodded. "Squeeze play," he said.

A few minutes later, the Thunder earned a throw-in. Fivehead tossed ahead of Max on the flank. Max gathered the ball and looked up, Red and Eddie a few feet away. Max saw a window between them. He tried to slash through, but fell right into the trap. Red and Eddie hit Max from both sides. With six legs clustered over the ball, Red snuck a knee into Max's thigh.

As Max sank to the turf, Eddie dribbled down the flank, Red dashing toward goal. Max stood and tried to run, but the knot in his leg pounded. He watched Eddie loft the ball into the box. Theo surged out, his hands up. "Keeper's ball!"

But it wasn't. Red came out of nowhere. He leaped over Theo and snapped his head into the ball. The ball clanged the bar and bounced back to Red. This time, he headed the rebound clean into the open net.

Red sprinted off. As he neared the Thunder bench, he dove and slid to a stop six feet from Coach Pepper. As Red got mobbed by his teammates, Coach ran out to Max.

"Got kneed in the thigh, really hurts."

Coach and Fivehead helped Max to the bench. A minute later, the ref blew the final whistle. Lightning 2, Thunder 1.

Max sat, a towel draped over his face. His teammates shook hands with the Lightning players, but Max didn't move. His mom and dad came over. They offered to help Max to the car, but he waved them off. Max stood and limped toward the lot. At the end of the handshake line, Coach Pepper met Red. Red let a sly grin play across his face. "I told ya, Coach, you shoulda kept me in the middle."

Coach Pepper squeezed Red's hand, squeezed it hard. "I saw what you did to Max," Coach said. "You got away with it today. You won't the next time." Red smirked and walked off.

Max and his parents reached the car.

"What happened to your leg?" his mom asked.

"Red kneed my thigh. Pretty sneaky, the ref missed it."

"That kid's a rat," Betsy snapped. "Three guys tangled up, he knew it was his chance to take you out."

Mr. Miles eyed Max in the rear-view mirror. "I liked the way you tried that bicycle kick."

"Yeah, but I still got work to do," Max muttered.

"Your birthday is coming up," his dad replied. "I have an idea for a present."

"What's that?" Max asked.

"Keep getting 'A's on your report card, and you'll see," Mr. Miles answered.

At home Max's leg tightened up, and it was

sore in the morning. Mrs. Miles took him to the doctor. The news was not good. Max had a severe bruise, no soccer for ten days. On the way back to the car, he booted a rock off the sidewalk. "Ten days, that's gonna feel like ten months. I can't play against the Torpedoes on Saturday. If we don't beat them, we'll probably miss out on the championship game in Philadelphia."

"Your teammates will come through, Max," his mom said. "You know they want another shot at Red Peters."

On Saturday Max showed up at the field in jeans and a sweatshirt. The Thunder created chances, but with each shot they took, the goal seemed to shrink. Fivehead and Ben sprayed balls high and wide – or right into the keeper's chest. As the second half ticked down in a scoreless battle, Max tapped his sneakers on the grass. *Looks like we can kiss Philadelphia goodbye.*

In the final minute, Fivehead stole a pass and led Ben on the flank. Fivehead broke into the box and Ben rolled the ball ahead of him. Fivehead ran on and cracked a bolt. The keeper dove and got his fingers on the ball. It hit the far post and bounced in the goalmouth. Ben had followed the shot. He lunged at the ball from one side, a defender from the other. Ben got his toes on it first. As he fell, he watched the ball trickle across the line. Thunder 1, Torpedoes 0.

"Way to go, Ben!" Max screamed. The Thunder fought off the Torpedoes and hung on for the win. Coach Pepper called the boys in. "My word for the day is 'PERSISTENT.' It means, 'sticking to your goal even when the going gets tough.' When Fivehead shot, Ben didn't relax, he stayed on his task. He followed the ball and got his toes on it before the defender did."

"Coach, that goal was so lame, I was almost embarrassed," Ben cracked.

The boys laughed, but Coach put up a hand. "Your toes won the game, Ben, that's all that matters."

Coach turned to Max. "How's your leg?"

"Pretty sure it's healed, can't wait to practice on Wednesday."

"That's good news, Max. We need you to get to Philadelphia."

When Max got home, he checked the league standings.

Team	W-L-T	Pts
Lightning	4-0-1	13
Hornets	3-1-1	10
Thunder	3-1-1	10
Flash	2-1-2	8
Cheetahs	2-1-2	8
Fury	2-2-1	7
Rampage	1-3-1	4
Torpedoes	1-3-1	4
Dragons	1-4-0	3
Volcanoes	1-4-0	3

Wow, the Hornets keep winning. Next, he checked the leading scorers.

Player	Team	Goals	Assists	Pts
Peters	Lightning	9	4	22
Miles	Thunder	6	3	15
Stoneman	Hornets	6	3	15
Hazard	Lightning	6	2	14
Robertson	Fury	4	3	11

Red leads the league, how did that happen? A new message came in, and Max opened it.

Lightning wins the league, Peters wins the scoring title. You lose.

Max thought about what to write back. Then he decided – nothing. *I'm not going to waste any more energy on Red Peters.*

On Monday night, the Miles family celebrated Max's twelfth birthday. His mom and Betsy made his favorite dinner – deep dish pepperoni pizza. He gobbled up two slices, topped off with a chocolate sundae. After dinner, Max took on his family in a game of Yahtzee. He finished last. "So much for birthday luck," he said.

Mr. Miles stood. "I just won Yahtzee, Max, but you get the big prize today. Come out to the deck, I have something to show you."

Max followed his parents and Betsy through the sliding doors. Following his dad's gaze past the Square, he saw a trampoline, surrounded by netting six feet high. "Dad, that's awesome!" Max yelped.

"Perfect place to practice your bicycle kick," his dad said.

"You know it!" Max grabbed a ball out of the bin and jogged to the trampoline.

"Go easy on your leg," his dad called.

Max climbed on, bounced the ball, and

watched it rise overhead. When the ball reached its apex, he jumped and leaned back. Swinging his left leg up, Max snapped his right foot into the falling ball. *Wham!* Max made solid contact, but the ball flew over the netting and into the bushes. *Need to work on my angle.* Max retrieved the ball and hit six more, but only two clean. *Okay, one more.* This time he imagined the ball was Red's face. *Thunk!* He cracked his best shot yet.

Later that night, Max and Betsy watched 'Victory,' a movie about Pele, the greatest soccer player ever. Growing up in Brazil, Pele had no money for cleats or a ball. He played barefoot in the streets and on the sand, with a ball made of rags tied together. Max was in awe of the way Pele dribbled, *tap, tap, tap,* the ball never more than a step away.

Max was also amazed to learn that Pele was the most famous athlete in the world. Pele was so popular that he even stopped a war. In 1967, he and his team flew from Brazil to Nigeria to play two exhibition matches. There was one problem: Nigeria was fighting a war against the rebels of Biafra. But both armies were excited to see Pele play, and they agreed to halt the war for a few days. After the matches were played, Pele and his team returned to Brazil, and the fighting started again.

As the movie ended, Mr. Miles stepped in. "So, Max, I just ran into Coach Pepper at the supermarket. He told me he has a special guest coming to your practice Tuesday."

"Who is it?" Max asked.

"No idea, he wouldn't tell me."

Later that night, Max leafed through his social studies notebook. He still hadn't decided what to do with his two big projects — his paper on a global trend and his project on a wall. He had two weeks before his paper was due, four weeks until he presented on walls with Red. He tugged at his hair. *I gotta come up with something soon, cuz the walls are closing in on me.*

CHAPTER 8

ONE FOOT, EIGHT WEAPONS

A T PRACTICE ON TUESDAY, MAX was warming up when he heard a car roar into the parking lot. A man got out of a red sports car. He wore black from head to toe – black ball cap, T-shirt, shorts, socks, and boots. The man jogged over. Coach gave him a hug, and then he called the players in.

"Boys, this is my friend, Gary Ball," Coach said. "Gary is coach of the Falcons, the state's top under-thirteen academy team. He offered to come by and give you some tips."

The boys introduced themselves by name, and then Coach Gary stepped forward. "So lads, I hear you're all good footballers," he said, his English accent thick.

"We call it soccer," Fivehead blurted, "but you got a cool accent. You from England?"

"I was born and raised in England, just like the game of soccer."

Fivehead tilted his head sideways. "Say what?"

"The English invented soccer about a thousand years ago," Coach Gary explained. "As people moved out of England to other parts of the world, they took soccer with them. That's how it became so popular, all over the globe."

When Max heard the word "globe," an idea hit him like a bolt from the sky. *Soccer is a global trend that changed the world. I'll do my social studies paper on soccer!*

Coach Gary flicked up a ball and caught it. "Okay, lads, a quick quiz. How many parts of the foot can you use in soccer?"

Ben put up his hand. "Three – the instep, the outside, and the inside."

Max added three more. "The toes, the heel, and the bottom."

"You lads are good," Coach said. "Six down, two to go. Watch this."

Coach Gary punted the ball straight up. As it neared the ground, he raised his leg and cushioned the ball on the crown of his foot. "The top," called out Chipper.

"That's seven," Coach Gary said. "Now, here's eight." Coach dribbled toward the boys and cocked his leg, as if he was about to smash the ball at them. As the boys shielded their faces, Coach slowed his kicking leg. Using the outside of his big toe, he tapped the ball behind his other leg. Max's jaw fell open. *That was cool.*

Coach did the move again. "That's called the Cruyff turn, named for the great Dutch player, Johan Cruyff. You use the bone below your big toe to tap the ball behind your other leg. Very tricky, almost impossible to defend."

Coach Gary flicked the ball into his hands. "So that's eight weapons on each foot. Now, how many of you are right-footed?" Every boy but Theo put up a hand. "Okay," Coach asked, "anyone have a really good left foot?"

Max started to raise his hand, but when no other hands went up, he scratched his head instead. Coach Gary frowned. "That's what I figured. Look, you need to work on your weak foot. Don't be the boy who uses his left foot only to get on the bus."

Artie put up a hand. "Coach, my dad says

that some of the world's best players used only one foot. Maradona was all left foot, Franz Beckenbauer was all right foot."

"That's true, Artie, but those are rare exceptions. With two good feet, you can move the ball in any direction. You can dribble, pass, and shoot, no matter where the ball sits."

Next, Coach pointed at his head. "What's this for?"

"To head the ball," Ben answered.

"Right, but what else?"

"To think," Max said.

"Bingo!" Coach Gary yelled. "The best players are great thinkers. Your games last eighty minutes, but you have the ball at your feet for less than two minutes. That leaves you seventy-eight minutes to help your teammates."

Max glanced at Fivehead, who was yanking grass out of the ground. "Coach, I hate to pop your balloon, but this is a soccer field, not a classroom."

"Cannon!" bellowed Coach Pepper. "Go sit by the goal."

Fivehead got up and dragged his feet down the field.

"Sorry about that, Gary," Coach Pepper said. "Carry on."

Coach Gary pointed toward the sideline. "Max, dribble a ball to that line."

Max dribbled to a line thirty yards away. Coach looked at his watch. "When I say 'go,' dribble past me as fast as you can. Go!"

Max took off, pushing the ball with the outsides of his feet until he sailed past Coach. Coach checked his watch. "Six seconds. Now go back."

Max returned to the line. "Now pass to me, hard and low," Coach said. Max did. Coach controlled it and checked his watch. "Two seconds."

Coach eyed the players. "Boys, two is much better than six. Passing is the essence of good soccer. When your teammate has the ball, don't watch, move. Be a target."

Coach Gary's watch beeped. "I've got a few more minutes. Coach Pepper, can Fivehead rejoin us?"

Coach Pepper looked toward the goal. Fivehead was hanging upside-down from the crossbar, his arms dangling near the ground. "Cannon, get down from there, and get over here!"

Fivehead dropped and ran over. Coach Pepper glared. "What are you, some monkey?"

Fivehead put his hands up. "I was just hangin' around."

"Very funny, Cannon. I woulda left you hangin', but Coach Gary invited you back."

Coach Gary dug into his jacket pocket and pulled out an index card. "I'm an English teacher, like Coach Pepper. I love words, especially words that have different meanings in America than they do in England."

Fivehead tossed his head back. "You gotta be kidding, Coach. I go to soccer practice, and I end up in English class?"

"Cannon!" Coach Pepper wailed.

"Sorry!"

"My first word is the game you play," Coach Gary said. "Soccer is called football everywhere except in America. Think about it. You use your feet much more in soccer than you do in American football." Max nodded. *I never thought about that.*

Coach checked his card. "In England, a truck is called a lorry."

"Hey, that's my mom's name," Fivehead said. "Who knew she was a truck?"

The boys howled. Coach Gary pointed at Theo. "You see how Theo's hair falls over his forehead? What do we call that here?"

"Bangs," Theo said.

"Right, but in England, we call it 'fringe.'"

Coach checked his list. "My next word is 'braces.'"

Fivehead pointed at Artie. "Artie just got braces. He likes Mary Simms, but she has braces, too. He's afraid that if they kiss, their braces might get stuck. Who wants to walk around school with a girl attached to your face?"

The boys hooted, but Artie shot back, "At least I'll have straight teeth, Fiver. You should get braces, unless you want to star in horror movies."

Coach Gary put up a hand to quiet the chuckles. "In England, braces hold up your pants. You call them suspenders."

Coach rolled on. "If you order fish and chips in England, what do you get?"

"Fish and potato chips?" Max guessed.

"Good try. In England, chips are french fries."

"What do they call potato chips?" Max asked.

"Crisps."

"Crisps?" Fivehead echoed. "I can barely say it. I mean, crisp rhymes with lisp."

Coach Gary's watch beeped again, and he picked up his bag. "Lads, I'm off to scout a player. His name is Red Peters. He scores a lot of goals, and I need a scorer for my state team. Good luck with your season."

As Coach Gary jogged off, Max's mouth hung open. *He's scouting Red Peters? I took Red's position, so why isn't he scouting me?*

Coach called the players in. Fivehead spoke. "Coach Gary's cool, but he's scouting Red Peters? What's an English word for, 'goofball?'"

Coach let his eyes rest on Max. "We keep winning, and Coach Gary might scout some of you."

At dinner that night, Max tore into a cheese enchilada. "How was practice?" Mr. Miles asked.

"Good and bad," Max replied. "The coach of the under-thirteen state team was there, taught us some cool stuff. But then he left to scout Red Peters, says he needs a scorer. Can you believe that?"

Mrs. Miles nodded. "Like I say, Max, scorers are hard to find."

"I know, maybe I need to score more."

"Maybe you do," she agreed.

Later that night, Max started his paper. He did a search on 'soccer history,' and soon he had filled three pages with notes. He began to write.

"Soccer was invented in England in the eleventh century. Whole villages would play against each other. For a ball, they would use the skull of a dead animal, or a pig's bladder. Players could use any part of their body to move the ball, even their hands. There were no goals. They would play across hills and streams until one team got the ball into the center of the other team's village. As people moved to other parts of the world, they took soccer with them."

Max wrote some more and counted up the words – 172. *Good start.* He changed into his pajamas, brushed his teeth, and climbed into bed. *So Coach Gary's looking for a scorer? Time to start piling up the goals.*

CHAPTER 9
TUNNEL VISION

"BRING IT IN, THUNDER!"

Coach Pepper's voiced boomed to the corners of Liberty Park Field. Max and his teammates huddled around their leader. Coach shook his fists. "Win every free ball. Keep the ball moving, keep it on the floor. Hands in." The players stacked hands on top of Coach's. "Three, two, one – THUNDER!"

As Max took the field, he eyed the goal he would be attacking. *I'm gonna have a big day, can feel it in my cleats.* Two minutes in, Max picked off a pass near the circle and burst ahead. When two defenders closed, Max squeezed between them. As he neared the box, he glanced up and saw the keeper edging out. *Time for a rainbow.*

Max stubbed his boot under the ball and

watched it rise. The keeper scrambled back and leaped, but the ball cleared his fingers and ducked under the bar. Thunder 1, Flash 0. Max punched at the sky. *That's one, Coach Gary.*

Minutes later, Flash twins Biff and Teddy Shuckers worked a give-and-go around Chipper. Biff ripped a hard shot from twenty yards, but Theo snared it on a short hop. He hurled wide to Charlie, who flicked to Max in the circle. Max spun into open space and quickly scanned his options. "Fiver, go corner." Fivehead bolted down the flank. Max pulled his leg back. His opponent lunged, and Max tapped the ball between his boots.

"Go, Max!" Betsy yelled.

Max pushed the ball ahead and looked up. *I got an open lane into the box.* As Max neared the box, he saw Fivehead dart free to his right. Max faked a pass, cut left, and fired from twenty yards. Flash defender Mick Farrell got a boot on the shot, deflecting it over the line.

"Max, I was open," Fivehead called.

"I had a shot," Max replied.

"Okay, but look for me."

Five minutes later, Chipper swept up a loose ball and led Max with a long ball down the flank. As Max collected near the edge of the box, Chipper broke free toward the back post, his hand up. Max tapped once and lashed a drive that sailed over the bar.

Chipper ran up. "You had me, Max." Max nodded, but said nothing. Minutes later Max flagged a stray pass in the circle. He blew past a defender and saw Ben breaking free to his left. Ben called for the ball, but Max had his sights set on the frame. From thirty yards he cranked a stinger, but the ball flew into the keeper's hands.

This time, Ben got in Max's face. "I was in alone!" he snapped.

Max nodded. "I'll get you next time, Ben."

Mr. Miles left the sideline and walked up to join Mrs. Miles and Betsy in the stands. "Max is trying to do it all himself," he said.

"It's like he forgot how to pass," Betsy added.

"He probably could pass more," Mrs. Miles admitted.

Betsy rolled her eyes. "Ya think, Mom?"

The ref blew his whistle to signal halftime. The Thunder huddled by their bench. Before

Coach Pepper could speak, Artie blurted, "Max is hogging the ball."

Max glared at Artie, but Fivehead piled on. "Max, they got guys all over you. I'm wide open."

Coach eyed Max. "You can't dribble around ten guys, Max. Your teammates are getting open, you've got to feed them."

Max nodded, but inside he burned. *Coach says I'll score a bunch. Now he yells at me for trying to score?*

At the start of the second half, Max took the tap from Fivehead, cut around one foe, and broke like a blur down the right flank. "Max, now!" Ben called as he sped toward the box. Max faked a cross and slipped the ball between his mark's legs. "Stop him!" screamed the Flash coach. As two defenders closed on Max, Fivehead darted toward the corner. Max saw him, but he tried to split the defenders. One boy got a boot on the ball, sending Max crashing to the turf. "Where's the call, ref?" Max pleaded from his knees.

"He got the ball first!" yelled the ref.

In the stands, Mr. Miles dug his fingers

into his forehead. "Max is playing one against eleven."

Betsy nodded. "If Coach Pepper had longer hair, he'd be pulling it out."

A bit later, Biff Shuckers dribbled around Chipper into space near the top of the box. He slid a lateral pass to his brother Teddy, free on the right. Teddy smashed a low drive that eluded Theo's reach and caromed in off the far post. Thunder 1, Flash 1.

Inspired by their goal, the Flash took control. They attacked in waves, forcing Theo to parry a barrage of shots. With only seconds left in the game, Theo corralled a cross and hurled wide to Chipper. Max knew this might be his last chance. He broke for the corner, and Chipper floated the ball ahead of him. Max collected on the run and cut in toward the box. Fivehead ran free to Max's left. "Max, now!" he called.

But Max only had eyes for the goal. He dribbled around one player and cut deeper toward the line. Running out of room, he tried to chip back to Fivehead, but a defender hustled back and headed the ball clear. The ref blew the final whistle, ending the 1-1 deadlock.

When Max got to the sideline, he had a

bullseye on his forehead. "Miles, you blew it!" Artie ranted. Fivehead piled on. "I was open the whole second half, but you didn't pass once. Guess you didn't listen to Coach."

"Enough!" hollered Coach Pepper. He scratched his head, searched for words. "Theo, great job in goal, you kept us in it. You had to, because we were horse manure today."

Coach fixed his stare on Max. "Max, you tried to take on the world today. That's not how the game is played, you know that."

As Max scraped his boot on the turf, the chatter grew. Coach put up his hand. "Boys, my word is 'COLLABORATE.' It means 'work together.' In soccer, you must think first about your teammates. The best players don't win, the best team wins. Now go home and think about that."

Max started for his bag, but he didn't make it. "Miles, come here," Coach snapped. Max walked back, his eyes on his laces. Coach dropped a hand on his shoulder. "I don't know what got into you today. You had guys open, but you didn't pass."

"I thought I had chances to score."

"Your teammates had better chances,"

Coach fired back. "Next week, I want to see the real Max Miles."

Max nodded. He trudged toward the parking lot, where his family waited. "Tough game, son," Mr. Miles said.

"Coach said I hogged the ball."

"You didn't pass like you usually do," Mr. Miles replied.

"I had some good looks, my shot just wasn't on."

"You had guys open," Betsy cut in.

"But I'm the scorer on this team, right?" Max fired back.

"You don't have to score every time you get the ball," his mom said.

Great, now my mom says I shoot too much. My mom!

Later that night, Max got out his notebook and scanned his to-do list. His social studies report was due a week from Friday. He opened his notes and picked up where he left off.

"Today soccer is the most popular sport in the world. Every four years, hundreds of countries

from all over the globe compete to win the World Cup. The World Cup is watched by more people than any other sports event, even the Olympics. When a country's team plays a World Cup match, the streets are empty because everyone is watching the game."

Max wrote on until he finished the draft. He counted the words – 332. *Made it!*

As Max put the draft on his desk, a note caught his eye. WALL PROJECT. He flopped on his bed, ran his eyes around his room. *I gotta find a topic soon, or my back's gonna be against the wall.*

Later, Max got on the computer and checked the standings.

Team	W-L-T	Pts
Lightning	5-0-1	16
Hornets	4-1-1	13
Thunder	3-1-2	11
Flash	2-1-3	9
Fury	2-2-2	8
Cheetahs	2-3-1	7
Rampage	1-3-2	5
Torpedoes	1-3-2	5

| Volcanoes | 1-4-1 | 4 |
| Dragons | 1-4-1 | 4 |

Looks like Red and Eddie are going to Philadelphia. But we gotta catch the Hornets. Next, he hit the 'Leading Scorers' tab.

Player	Team	Goals	Assists	Pts
Peters	Lightning	11	4	26
Miles	Thunder	7	3	17
Hazard	Lightning	6	4	16
Stoneman	Hornets	6	4	16
Robertson	Fury	5	4	14

Max's phone dinged, a message from Red. *"Hey loser, what'd I tell you? I'm gonna be playin' for the Falcons next year. You're gonna be stuck in a Thunderstorm! Go back to New Jersey, you wimp!"*

Max got up and booted his tennis ball into the wall. *Coach Gary must want Red. But that's bull, I beat Red out.*

Max looked at the scoring leaders again. *I gotta win the scoring title. I'm four behind with three games to play. Time to go on a tear, starting next Saturday against the Dragons.*

CHAPTER 10
TAKING A SEAT

THAT WEEK IN CLASS, MAX nearly filled an entire notebook. Not with notes, with soccer doodles. Over and over, he scratched out a goal and drew lines curling into the corners. Riding the bus home on Friday, he counted seventeen pages of his soccer artwork. Max smiled. *You scored all week on paper. Tomorrow, you gotta do it on grass.*

The next morning, Mr. Miles slid a plate of pancakes in front of Max. "Ready for the big game?"

Max nodded. "I feel a hat trick coming on, Dad."

Mr. Miles sat. "Remember, Max, three assists are as good as three goals. Make sure you pass the ball."

"I will," Max said as he drizzled syrup on his stack. "But you know I gotta catch Red Peters."

Mr. Miles fixed his eyes on Max. "I told you to forget about that kid."

"He's hard to forget when he's always in my face." Max gobbled his pancakes and went up to change. Betsy passed him on the stairs and joined Mr. Miles at the table. "Bets, I'm worried about Max," Mr. Miles said. "He's goal crazy."

"I hope he learned his lesson last week, but I'm not so sure," Betsy replied.

"Me neither," Mr. Miles said. "I'm taking my video camera to the game."

"Great idea, Dad!"

An hour later, Max opened the game with a tap to Fivehead. Max cut wide and zoomed down the flank, and Fivehead spooned a high ball toward the corner. Max gathered on the run and slithered past a defender. Fivehead raced into the box. "Far post!" he called.

Max saw Fivehead break free, but he could sniff the net. Surging into the box, he saw the keeper stray off his line. Max clipped the bottom third of the ball, sending a soft chip over the keeper. The keeper staggered back and leaped, but the ball arched over his hands and dipped under the bar. Thunder 1, Dragons 0. Max shook his fists. *That's one.*

Fivehead ran up and gave Max a high-five. But Fivehead wondered...*will Max ever pass to me again?*

A bit later Max stole a pass thirty yards from goal. As he built speed toward the only back between him and the goal, Fivehead burst free down the flank. "Max, now!" he called. "Fiver!" Max called out, but the back didn't buy it. Max tried to cut past, and the back jarred the ball away.

Fivehead ran to Max. "What's wrong with you?"

"Nothin', just play."

"Give me the ball, and I will!"

While Max and Fivehead sniped at each other, the Dragons had strung together three passes to set up striker Bart Mapes thirty yards from goal. Bart cut past Charlie and whacked a low drive. Theo dove, but swatted air. The ball flew clean into the corner, tying the game.

When the Thunder jogged off at halftime in a one-one draw, Coach Pepper met them with a scowl. "No way this team should hang with us, we gotta pass the ball!" Coach ran his eyes from player to player, stopping to focus on Max. "Here's the deal. If I see anyone hogging it in the second half, I'll bench him."

Max gulped his water and jogged back out. *Was Coach looking at me when he talked about hogging the ball? Nah, he's just hot because I haven't scored more.*

Early in the second half, Chipper led Fivehead into the circle. "Fiver!" Max called as he cut toward the box. Fivehead threaded the ball between two foes and onto Max's boot. Max turned to face the goal, two defenders closing in. Fivehead circled behind. "Lead me!" Fivehead called.

But Max had his eyes on the frame. He tried to squeeze between his foes, but one blasted the ball clear. "Max!" Coach Pepper hollered. He looked at his bench. "Scott, get loose."

A minute later Max plucked the ball from a thicket of legs in the circle and burst toward goal. He juked around one defender, setting up a three-on-two with Fivehead to his right, Ben to his left. "Now!" yelled Ben as he broke toward the box.

Max swung his foot back, but he didn't pass. He tried to split the defenders, but one tackled the ball and drilled it up the flank. The horn sounded. "Substitution!" yelled the referee's assistant. Scott Parker jogged toward Max. "You're out."

Max's mouth fell open. "Me?"

"Yup, you."

His head hung, Max began to walk off. "Move it, eleven!" the ref called out.

Max stepped into a jog. He realized this was the first time he had ever been taken out of a close game. Nearing the sideline, Max felt a surge of shame. But then he saw something that made him feel even worse. Sitting in the stands was Gary Ball, jotting notes on a clipboard. Max slumped on the bench and hung a towel on his head.

Scott gave the Thunder a boost. Nicknamed "Spider" for his long legs, he made a slide-tackle to strip the ball from his opponent. Seeing Fivehead sprint toward the far post, Scott launched a cross. The ball sailed over a crowd and started down toward Fivehead. He cushioned the ball on his chest. It popped up and started to drop. Fivehead drove his right boot into it. His powerful volley rose over the keeper's hands. *Thunk!* The ball rattled the far post and bounced all the way out of the box.

Dragon Lou Buckley outran Chipper to the ball. Spotting his striker Mark Bailey running through the circle, Lou launched a high ball into the Thunder's end. Mark, the fastest player in the league, raced past Charlie and closed in on the ball as it rolled toward the box. Theo bounced on his toes, unsure if he could beat Mark to the ball. He decided to go for it, but the lost time cost him. Mark got to the ball first and slammed a low drive into the net. Dragons 2, Thunder 1.

On the bench, Max stared at his laces. *Great, I get taken out and we give away the game.*

Now the Dragons had momentum. They attacked in waves, forcing Theo to make three diving saves. Chipper gave the Thunder one final flicker of hope with a gallant run down the left side, but his cross got caught up in the wind and the keeper snatched it. The final whistle blew. Dragons 2, Thunder 1.

As the Thunder gathered around Coach Pepper, Max tried to swallow off the lump in his throat. "I hope we learned a lesson today, boys," Coach said. "The Dragons do not have better players, but they were the better team. They passed and they hustled. That's why they won, and we lost."

Coach paced. "My word today is, 'UNDER-ACHIEVE.' It means you did not perform up to your full ability. Go home and think about that."

Max began to walk away, but he didn't get far. "Miles, hang on," Coach called out. Max froze, his eyes on the grass. Coach neared. "Know why I benched you? Because you tried to be a hero. You had teammates open, but you dribbled until you lost the ball."

Max kept his eyes on his boots. "I thought I had chances to score."

"You don't have to score, the team has to score," Coach volleyed. "The ball-hogging stops now, got it?"

Max nodded. He walked away, his eyes down until he met his dad and sister in the parking lot. "Coach said I hogged the ball."

"I shot video," Mr. Miles said. "We can watch the game at home."

"I'm good with that," Max said.

Later that afternoon, the Miles family gathered in the family room to watch the game. Mr. Miles was about to start the video when Max's phone beeped, an email from Red Peters. Max read it. "BENCHWARMER! LOSER!"

Max shook his head. *Red must have spies in the bushes.* Mr. Miles had already fast-forwarded ten minutes in. He hit the 'play' button. Max takes a pass from Fivehead, who runs free and calls for a pass back. But Max tries to split two defenders and loses the ball. Mr. Miles paused the video. Max put up his hands. "Okay, I shoulda passed there."

Mr. Miles hit fast-forward again, stopping when Fivehead feeds Max at the top of the box. Fivehead runs behind Max into open space, but Max bulls into two defenders and loses the ball. "That's twice," said Mr. Miles.

"Dad, when I get close, you tell me to attack the net."

"You had two defenders in front of you," Mr. Miles hit back. "A pass to Fivehead creates a better chance."

Mr Miles let the video run until Max leads a three-on-two break with Fivehead and Chipper at his sides. Max fakes a pass to Chipper and tries to barrel ahead, but the ball is swept off his boot. Mr. Miles shut off the video. "That's when Coach took you out."

Max slumped back, squeezed his eyes shut. Mrs. Miles spoke. "Max, you –"

"Hogged the ball," Max said, finishing her sentence. "I can't believe it. I guess I didn't know what I was doing."

Mrs. Miles hung an arm around him. "I owe you an apology, Max. I've been pushing you to score, and that's wrong. I won't do it anymore."

"That would help, Mom," Max said. "But here's the worst thing. I saw Coach Ball in the stands. He saw me get benched."

"Forget about Coach Ball," Mr. Miles snapped. "And forget about Red Peters. You let him lure you into a scoring contest, and that's when you stopped playing like Max Miles."

Max got up, but his dad wasn't done. "You need to apologize to your teammates, and to Coach Pepper."

"I'm gonna start with Fivehead," Max said.

Max went to his room and called Fivehead. "Fiver, it's Max. My Dad shot a video of our game. You were right, I hogged the ball, big time. Sorry."

"That wasn't you these last two games, Max, it was some imposter," Fivehead replied. "But forget about it. We're gonna win our next two games, still make Philadelphia."

"Sounds good, Fiver." Max hung up and slumped on his bed. *Saying sorry to Fiver wasn't so bad. But apologizing to Coach? That's gonna be brutal.*

CHAPTER 11

HERO WITH NO GOALS

MAX WOKE THE NEXT MORNING with his dream still clanking in his head. In it, he had apologized to Coach Pepper, and Coach had said, "Miles, you blew it. I'm benching you for the next game." Max pulled the sheet over his head. *I really messed up, against the worst team in the league. What if Coach keeps me on the bench?*

At the start of lunch period that day, Max headed for Coach's classroom. The door was open, but Coach wasn't there. Max tapped his toes on the carpet. *Should I write him a note?*

"Miles!" Coach barked from behind. Max jumped. "Hey, Coach."

Coach walked to his desk, sat, and waved Max into another chair. Coach swept a hand over the piles of paper scattered across the desk. "So Max, you like my filing system?"

Max snickered. Coach laced his fingers on the desk. "Okay, boy, you're not here to play tic-tac-toe. What's on your mind?"

Max cleared his throat. "Coach, my dad took a video of our game. You were right, I dribbled too much, sorry. "

Coach stuck out his hand, and Max shook it. "Max, I'm proud of you for owning up to your selfish play."

"I'm gonna apologize to the team at practice," Max added.

"Good idea."

Max felt his heart thud on his shirt. "Coach, will I be in the starting lineup on Saturday?"

Coach thumped a fist on his desk, and Max jerked in his chair. "Is a soccer ball round, Max? Of course you'll start! Look, you let Red Peters rattle you, and then Coach Ball. You thought you had to score a pot of goals, right?" Max nodded, and Coach went on. "Okay, so now you're back to being Max Miles. It's time to win our last two games, and go to Philadelphia and unplug the Lightning. Deal?"

Max smiled. "Sounds good, Coach."

Max noticed a photo on the wall behind Coach. It showed Coach sitting in a baseball stadium, above a huge green wall. Max pointed at the photo. "Cool picture."

"My cousin works at Fenway Park in Boston," Coach said. "He got me tickets to a Red Sox game last summer. I sat in the bleachers above the Green Monster, the most famous wall in sports."

Max took a closer look at the wall – and it hit him. *My wall project, I'll do it on the Green Monster!*

As Max got up, he noticed whiskers on Coach's face. "Coach, you growin' a beard?"

Coach rubbed his chin. "I'm not shaving until we win a game. Hope my beard will motivate you guys."

Coach saw Max fight off a grin. "You don't like my stubble, Miles?"

"I'm okay with it. But Fivehead might have something to say."

Coach shot back, "I'm sure he will, that little scalawag."

"Scalawag?" Max echoed.

"Rascal, imp, you get the picture, Miles."

Max hustled off to the cafeteria. He spotted

Fivehead and ran over. "Fiver, get this, Coach is growing a beard."

Fivehead's eyes grew wide. "Good for him, he finally figured out how to hide his face."

Later that afternoon, Max had his best social studies class yet. Red was out sick, so Max didn't have to deal with him. When Mrs. Dingle returned Max's paper on the history of soccer, he smiled at the "A-" written on top. He read her note: *Max, creative topic, but you could've written more about soccer's impact. How does it help countries to grow? How does it create jobs? Next time, think as broadly as you can.* Max nodded. He figured that was fair.

Near the end of class, Missus Dingle brought up the wall project. "Class, you present in two weeks," she said. "Raise your hand if you've picked a subject." Max stuck up his hand. *Thanks, Coach Pepper.*

An hour later, the Thunder gathered for practice. Coach called the players in. He ran his eyes across each boy, stopping on Max. "I think Max has something to say." Max took a deep breath. "Guys, I'm sorry about how I played the last two games. From now on, I'm gonna play right."

"Let's forget about it," Coach said. "It's time to focus on the Volcanoes and Hornets. If we beat 'em both, we still have a shot to make Philadelphia."

The boys howled, and then Fivehead spoke. "Coach, there is something we need to talk about."

Coach fixed his eyes on Fivehead. "And what would that be, Cannon?"

"It's your face. You need to wash off the dirt."

The players howled. Coach lunged at Fivehead but he darted away. "Look," Coach said, "you beat the Volcanoes on Saturday, and the whiskers come off."

Coach took a ball out of his bag. "Okay, we're gonna play three-touch. You know the rules – you can touch the ball three times, max, then someone else must touch it."

Fivehead swung his boot through the grass. "Come on, Whiskers, three-touch is soccer light." Coach glared at Fivehead. "This forces you to pass the ball, play as a team."

Coach handed out eight red pinnies and

eight yellow pinnies. He booted the ball into the circle and shouted, "Play!" A few seconds in, Max poked the ball free. A defender closed so he pushed the ball into space. As he neared the ball, he realized he could touch it only once more. Looking up, Max saw Ben breaking into space. He chipped over two players onto Ben's boot.

Coach blew his whistle. "Great soccer! Max had only one more touch, so he looked for an open teammate. Ben did his part, running free to be a target."

Coach looked at Fivehead. "Maybe we'll play three-touch against the Volcanoes."

Fivehead shot back, "Maybe I'll quit soccer and take up badminton."

The Thunder played three-touch for an hour before Coach blew his final whistle. "Good stuff, boys. Remember, when your teammate has the ball, don't stand and watch. Get open!"

At Liberty Park on Saturday, Max and Fivehead stepped into a warm-up lap. "I'll be lookin' for ya," Max said.

Fivehead nodded. *You better be.*

Three minutes in, Max intercepted a pass and charged up the middle. As he neared the top of the box, Max had only one defender to beat. Out of the corner of his eye, he saw Fivehead to his right. Max cocked his leg. As the defender lunged, he slid the ball into Fivehead's lane. Fivehead ran on and creamed a low dart into the far corner. He ran over and jumped on Max. "Great pass!"

A bit later, Ben plucked the ball out of a scrum and Max released down the flank. "Now!" Max yelled. Ben led Max toward the corner. Max took control near the flag, a defender closing fast. With little room to maneuver, Max wound up as if to cross. When the defender slid, Max slowed his leg and gently chipped the bottom of the ball. The ball popped over his foe, and Max was free and clear.

Max dribbled along the end line toward the near post. Looking up, he spotted Fivehead barreling toward the far post, Chipper running toward the arc. "Far post!" Max yelled, but it was a decoy. He played a low ball back into Chipper's path. Chipper laced a screamer. The keeper dove and got a hand on it, but the ball deflected off the bottom of the bar and kicked over the line. Thunder 2, Volcanoes 0.

Chipper ran over to Max. "Great feed, Max!"

Fivehead leaped on Max. "Dude, you're on fire!"

Four minutes later, Fivehead snapped his big forehead into Chipper's corner kick, putting the Thunder up, 3-0. Jogging off at halftime, Max saw his dad give him two thumbs up. The Thunder huddled around Coach Pepper. "Fellas, that is beautiful soccer," Coach blared, and then he pointed at Max. "Miles, great stuff, keep it up."

As the Thunder took the field for the second half, Fivehead huddled with Max. "Time to get you a goal, Max."

Max got his chance on the Thunder's next possession. Fivehead worked a give-and-go with Max, springing Fivehead free into space near the box. As Fivehead dribbled along the eighteen, Max cut behind him. Fivehead stepped over the ball and heeled it back to Max. Max collected, dribbled once, and unloaded.

The keeper didn't move, no point in it. The ball exploded off Max's boot and whistled toward the far corner. "Clank!" The shot rang the post and bounced into the goalmouth. An alert Fivehead had broken for goal, and he tucked home the rebound.

Max ran over. "Nice finish, Fiver."

"Great shot, Max. We're still gonna get you one."

In the closing minute, Max fed Ben wide and darted to the far side. Sizing up Ben's cross, Max figured this was his chance. He turned his back to goal, jumped, and leaned back. Flicking his left foot up, Max swung his right foot at the ball. He whiffed and landed with a thud.

Fivehead ran over and helped Max up. "Nice try, Max."

Max brushed dirt off his shorts. *That bicycle kick is easy on the trampoline, but hard in a game. When am I gonna hit one?*

The Thunder cruised to a 4-0 win. Coach Pepper called in his troops. "That was your best match of the season, boys. Miles, I've never seen you play better."

"Come on, Coach, I didn't score. And I muffed my bicycle kick."

"You set up three goals!" Coach bellowed. "My word for the day describes you, 'REDEEM.' It means you made up for previous wrongs."

Coach checked his phone, and a smile edged across his face. "Good news, boys, the Hornets tied today. If we beat them next week, we earn a spot in Philadelphia, and a rematch against Red, Eddie, and the Lightning. We ready to sting the Hornets?"

"YES!"

Max walked over to his parents. "Your passing was fabulous, Max," his dad raved.

"Thanks, wish I scored."

"You came within a whisker on that smash from the eighteen," Mrs. Miles said. "You hit that so hard, I thought the post might snap in half."

Max snorted at that. When he got home, he logged onto the league site and checked the standings.

Team	w-l-t	Pts
Lightning	6-0-2	20
Hornets	4-1-3	15
Thunder	4-2-2	14
Flash	3-2-3	12
Fury	3-3-2	11
Torpedoes	2-2-4	10
Cheetahs	2-4-2	8

Dragons	2-5-1	7
Volcanoes	2-5-1	7
Rampage	1-5-2	6

Next, he hit the 'Leading Scorers' tab.

Player	Team	Goals	Assists	Pts
Peters	Lightning	13	5	31
Miles	Thunder	8	8	24
Hazard	Lightning	7	5	19
Stoneman	Hornets	6	5	17
Robertson	Fury	5	5	15

Wow, Red's way ahead. Guess I can forget about catching him.

Still in his uniform, Max went downstairs, grabbed a ball, and stepped outside. He climbed on the trampoline and smashed ten bicycle kicks with each foot. After the last one, he dropped on his back and stared into the blue sky. Closing his eyes, Max imagined himself drilling a bicycle kick into the corner against the Hornets.

When Max got back to his room, he saw a message on his phone. *Hey dork, I hope you beat the Hornets. Then we get to play you in Philadelphia,* and you know what happens then? You get torched by a bolt of lightning! Can't wait to ruin your season, and ruin Coach Pepper's season!

Max typed back. *Don't worry, Red, we'll beat the Hornets. Then it's payback time.*

CHAPTER 12

THUNDER VERSUS HORNETS...
WHO GETS STUNG?

SITTING IN HIS LAST CLASS the following Friday, Max kept looking at the clock on the wall. *That second hand is ticking in slow motion, I swear.*

Finally, Saturday came. When Max got to the park, he jogged to the bench and stepped into a warm-up lap with Fivehead. Max set a fast pace. "Max, you gotta slow down," Fivehead whined.

Max eased up. "Sorry, Fiver, I'm so pumped up."

"I get it, but save some sting for the Hornets."

"Don't worry, Fiver, nothin's gonna stop me today."

In the pre-game huddle, Coach Pepper took

a few seconds to lock eyes with each player. "Boys, we have to win this game. If we tie or lose, the Hornets finish second, and our fall season is over." Coach put out a hand, and the boys stacked theirs on top. "Three, two, one, THUNDER!"

From the opening whistle, Max was a marked man. Wherever he went, two Hornets followed. Max caught a shoulder here and an elbow there, but he worked hard to get free and flicked off some good passes. The Hornets' back line held firm, and the game stayed scoreless late into the first half.

When the Thunder earned a corner kick, Max retreated thirty yards from goal. The two players marking him stayed in the box. Fivehead lashed his kick toward the goalmouth, and Max edged toward the eighteen. The keeper punched out the cross – right at Max. He took two steps and swung his right boot into the ball. *Thwack!* Max watched the ball rise like a rocket and snap the roof of the net. Thunder 1, Hornets 0.

In the stands, Mrs. Miles pumped her fist. "That ball was smoked!" she crowed.

Betsy nodded. "Max was smart to stay out of

the box. No sense tryin' to shake off two guys close to goal."

At halftime, the Thunder trotted off with a one-goal lead. "Boys, we're forty minutes from Philadelphia," Coach said. "Let's pass and possess. Don't get too defensive, we'll just invite them back in it."

But the Hornets had their sights on Philadelphia, too. Knowing they needed a goal, they moved a defender up to midfield. Two minutes in, Hornets striker Ben Davis cracked a missile that Theo tipped inches over the bar. Coach Pepper waved Max over. "They're pushing more people forward," Coach said. "You need to think defense first."

Minutes later the Hornets earned a corner kick. Max took his spot at the back post. The kick flew in. Ben Davis soared high at the penalty spot and headed the ball toward the back corner. Max jumped. The ball hit the top of his head, caromed into the bar, and bounced on the line. As a Hornet neared, Max jumped and scissor-kicked the ball out of the box.

"Great play, Max!" yelled Mr. Miles from the sideline. Max looked that way. *Wow, Dad never yells during a game, he is so jacked up.* As the clock wound down, the Hornets attacked like waves rolling onto the beach. After Ben Davis lashed a shot just over the bar, Max looked over at his dad. Mr. Miles held up four fingers. *Man, I hope we can hold on.*

Seconds later, the Hornets earned another corner. As the ball curled in, Chipper rose high and snapped into a powerful header that flew out of the box. As the ball bounced toward the circle, Hornet center back Jeff Puddle ran up and swung into a wicked smash that knuckled high and far. Theo backpedaled and put up his hands. The ball ticked his fingers and struck the post. Max lunged for it, but Ben Davis got a boot in first. The ball squirted over the line, tying the match. Ben ran toward the corner flag and slid on his knees. The Hornets were three minutes from going to Philadelphia, the Thunder three minutes from going nowhere.

Max tapped the kickoff to Fivehead and ran into space. Fivehead wanted to feed Max, but he saw three Hornets smothering him. Spotting Ben running free down the right flank, Fivehead lofted the ball toward the corner. Ben gave chase, and Max broke into a sprint. With three Hornets still on his heels, Max saw Ben thump a cross, the wind pushing the ball away from goal. As Max neared the eighteen, he knew it was time. *Bicycle kick.* He turned his back to goal, leaped, and leaned back. He swung his left leg up and then stabbed his right boot at the sinking ball.

Thump! *I hit that pretty good*, Max thought as he crashed to the turf. He turned to see his shot arc over the keeper. *Get down, ball, get down!* The shot hit the bar and dropped in the goalmouth. Fivehead and a Hornet defender darted toward the ball. Fivehead got a toe on it. The ball nicked the far post, bounced twice on the line, and trickled in. Thunder 2, Hornets 1.

Fivehead sprang up and sprinted into Max's arms. "What a shot, Max!" Fivehead wailed.

"You finished it, Fiver, great hustle!"

A minute later the final whistle sounded. Thunder 2, Hornets 1. Max was bent over at midfield, too tired to move. Finally, he ambled toward the bench, where he joined his teammates around Coach. "Boys, you earned this," Coach said, his voice hoarse. "When they tied it, you showed your mettle."

Coach nodded toward the Hornets' bench. "Let's shake hands." When Max reached the end of the line, the Hornets' coach pulled him aside. "You were the difference today. You played great at both ends."

"Thanks, Coach. You have an awesome team."

"One more thing," the Hornets' coach added. "That bicycle kick, wow, that was fabulous."

Max beamed. Coach Pepper called the team back in. "Boys, where are we going next Saturday?"

"PHILADELPHIA!" Coach reached in his bag, took out a stack of paper, and shook it. "I like to plan ahead, boys. This sheet has some fun facts on Philadelphia. Before our game we'll walk part of the city, visit some famous places. I expect you to show your parents how smart you are."

Fivehead put up a hand. "Coach –"

"Can it, Cannon."

Max got his bag and walked toward his family. His dad wrapped an arm around him. "Max, you were doubled up all game, but you worked your tail off."

"That bicycle kick was crazy good, Max," Mrs. Miles added.

"I still can't get one on goal."

"You got it on the wood, though," Betsy said, "and Fivehead was alert enough to finish it."

As they reached the car, a bright sun beamed down. "I have an idea," Mr. Miles said. "Let's celebrate with a trip to the beach."

"Deal!" Max yelled.

As Mr. Miles steered the van onto the highway an hour later, Max eyed the temperature gauge on the dashboard. "It may be late October, but it's seventy-seven degrees out. I'm hittin' the ocean."

"I'll beat you to it," Betsy fired back.

Mrs. Miles looked up from her crossword puzzle. "I need help with a clue. It's, 'not one goal but three.'"

"How many letters?" Max asked.

"Eight."

Max thought for a bit. "Hat trick?"

His mom studied the boxes. "That's it!"

"Why is scoring three goals called a hat trick?" Betsy asked.

"Good question," Mr. Miles said. "Can you name the sport where the term 'hat trick' was first used?"

"Ice hockey?" Max guessed.

"Try cricket."

"Cricket?" Max repeated. "That's not a sport, it's a bug."

"It is a sport, popular in England, Australia, and Asia," Mr. Miles said. "A bowler throws a ball at three upright sticks, which are called a wicket. If the bowler hits the wicket, the batter is out. When a bowler would hit three wickets in a row, his team would give him a hat as a gift. That's how 'hat trick' got started."

Max said, "Dad, you bowl me over with your knowledge."

Mrs. Miles finished the puzzle and got out a notepad. "Let's see how many different states we can see on license plates." Traffic was heavy, and the list quickly grew: New Jersey, Pennsylvania, New Hampshire, Maryland, Vermont, Delaware, North Carolina, Ohio. "We have eight already, bet we can get to twenty," Mrs. Miles said.

"I'll give ten dollars to anyone who sees Alaska," Mr. Miles cracked.

Max spied four more state plates before he felt his eyes closing. He leaned against the window and dozed off. When he woke, his dad was pulling up by the beach. Max gazed out at the dark green surf, made choppy by a stiff breeze. "Check out those waves!" Max blared.

Max and Betsy were already in their swim gear. They bolted out of the car and dashed toward the ocean. When Max reached the sand, he peeled off his T-shirt and kicked off his flip-flops without breaking stride. He hit the surf and kept running until the water reached his thighs. Max dove, but forgot to keep his mouth closed. He came up and spat out a mouthful. *Man, I feel like I just gargled with salt water.*

Max stared far off to where the sea met the sky. Even with the sun beating on him, he felt a chill from the water. *No wonder there aren't many people in the ocean.* He looked at the beach. A soccer game had started up, five boys playing against four. The boys looked about Max's age. He jogged onto the sand.

"Hey, you wanna play?" a boy called out. Max nodded, and the boy told him to put on a shirt. Max ran back, toweled off, and fished out his T-shirt. Mr. Miles looked up from his book. "How's it going?" he asked.

Max didn't bother to respond. He ran over and joined the game. The ball came his way.

Max started to dribble, but he stumbled and kissed the sand. "Sand's deep," said a kid with stringy blonde hair. "Take short steps. You don't sink in as far."

The boy stuck out his hand. "I'm Danny." Max shook. "I'm Max."

Max and Danny worked a one-two, Max slamming the return ball between two shirts set up as goalposts. As Max backpedaled into position, an idea hit him. *The sand is soft and deep – perfect for bicycle kicks.* A bit later Max's teammate floated a high ball his way. Max jumped, leaned back, flicked his left foot forward and then smashed his right foot into the ball. He met the ball clean, drilling a line drive into the chest of an opposing player. The ball ricocheted all the way into the surf. "Wow!" Danny said, "how did you do that?"

"I practice on my trampoline," Max said. "Usually don't hit 'em that good."

Over the next hour, Max tried four overhead kicks. Two he hit well, and two he muffed. *At least I'm getting better.* When the game broke up, Max walked back and grabbed a water bottle. In one tilt, he guzzled all sixteen ounces. "Aaaah, much better."

Mr. Miles tossed Max the sports section from *The Chelsea Chimes*. "Check out that ad," he said.

Soccer Tryouts, Pennsylvania Falcons
State Select Team – u-13 boys
November 8, 10 a.m.
King of Prussia Memorial Park
To sign up, email Coach Ball:
gball@falcons.com

"Dad, state tryouts for the Falcons. That's Coach Gary's team!"

Max started to stretch. "What are you doing?" Mr. Miles asked.

"Gonna take a jog up the beach, need to keep my lungs in shape."

"Forget that," Mr. Miles said. "You played a game this morning, and you just played pick-up for an hour. That's more than enough for one day. Why don't you write Coach Ball?"

Max got out his phone and began to write.

Dear Mr. Ball: My name is Mxx Miles. We met when you came to a Chelsea Thunder practice. I think you saw one of our games, too. I'd like to try out for your team. Thanks, Max

Max proofread the note, fixed the typo in his name, and hit 'send.'

When Max got home that night, he checked his to-do list for school. His wall presentation with Red was only four days away. He had practiced a few times in front of his mirror. Now it was time to present to his family.

After dinner, the Miles' gathered in the family room. "Okay, Max, tell us about the Green Monster," Mr. Miles said. Max stood, index cards in hand. He sailed through in three minutes. Only once did he pause for a bit, and that was because his cards were out of order. When he finished, he got a standing ovation.

"That was really good, Max," Betsy said.

"I really liked the bit about the scoreboard," Mr. Miles added.

Max looked at his mom. "Okay, Mom, what can I do better?"

"Remember to share your eyes, Max. After you read a sentence, pause and look up at the students."

Max nodded. *Mom's always got some advice. But this time, I think she's right.*

Later that night, Max was napping on the couch when the beep of his phone woke him. He saw an email, from Coach Gary. His heart beating fast, he sat up and read:

Dear Max: Thanks for your note. I'm sorry to tell you that my team is pretty well set. I did see you play against the Dragons. You're a talented player, but you hold the ball too long for this level. Keep working on your game.

Sincerely, Coach Ball

Max pitched his phone into the couch, just as his mom walked in. "What's up?" she asked.

"Coach Ball wrote me back, said I'm a ball hog." Max got up and stormed out. "Hang on," Mrs. Miles called out. But Max was in no mood to talk. He stomped upstairs and slammed his door shut. *I can't believe it, Coach Ball sees my worst game. He doesn't want me!*

Max's phone beeped again. *Hey Miles, I'm so glad you beat the Hornets. Now I get to bury you in Philadelphia on Saturday. Coach Ball will be there, checking me out. I'm gonna put on a show for him. Get ready to suck grass, punk.*

Max deleted the email, and then a smile crossed his face. *So Coach Ball will be at our game. This time, I'll show him the real Max Miles.*

CHAPTER 13

RED PETERS, THE GREEN MONSTER

ON HIS WAY TO SOCIAL studies class that Friday, Max could feel his heart hammer on his chest. *I gotta stand next to Red for five minutes. I'd rather be in the principal's office.*

Halfway through class, Mrs. Dingle called on Max and Red. They walked separate paths to the front. Their eyes never met. Red went first. "The Great Wall of China is the longest structure ever built by humans. It's thirteen thousand miles long. It could stretch across the United States five times. The wall was built over two thousand years ago, and is made of stone, brick and wood. It was built to protect the Chinese from being invaded."

When Red finished, Mrs. Dingle asked him why he chose the Great Wall. "Easy, Missus

Dingle. The Great Wall is the greatest wall ever, and I'm gonna be the greatest soccer player ever." A chorus of "boos" bounced off the walls.

Max was next. "I chose a baseball wall, the Green Monster at Fenway Park, home of the Boston Red Sox." Max paused and shifted his eyes to the other side of the room. "The Green Monster is the nickname for the wall in left field. It's thirty-seven feet high, the tallest wall in baseball. The wall was built so that fans could not watch games for free from the streets and restaurants behind left field. It was painted green in nineteen forty-seven, and that's when it became known as, 'the Green Monster.'"

Max went on. "Here's another cool fact: the wall has one of the few scoreboards that is not electronic. Workers keep score by hand. They sit in seats behind the wall and slide numbered tiles onto the scoreboard."

After Max finished, Mrs. Dingle asked him why he chose the Green Monster. Max shrugged. "I saw a picture of it on the wall in Coach Pepper's classroom."

Students roared, and Mrs. Dingle put up her hand. "Max, you saw your wall on a wall, pretty cool. I've been doing this project for fifteen years. You're the first student to present on the Green Monster, very creative."

As Max returned to his seat, Mrs. Dingle faced the class. "We just learned about the Great Wall and the Green Monster. Any comments?" Ben Kwan stuck up his hand. "The Green Monster reminds me of Red." Every student turned to face Ben.

"How so, Ben?" Mrs. Dingle asked.

"Well, green is the color of envy, and envy is another word for jealousy," Ben said. Then Ben looked at Red. "When it comes to soccer, Max owns Red. He turns Red into a green monster."

A few students snickered, and then the room fell silent. Red glared at Ben. "You little punk, Kwan. I'm gonna pummel you on Saturday."

Chatter shot through the room.

"Settle down, kids!" Mrs. Dingle called out. When the bell rang, she told Red to stay behind. In the hall, Max caught up with Ben. "Ben, what you said about Red being a green monster, that was wild."

"Yeah, pretty funny. You see Missus Dingle? She put a hand over her smile."

"But the best part was Red's reaction," Max said. "His face matched his name."

On Saturday morning, a bright sun rose in the sky as the Miles family drove into Philadelphia. They parked in a garage and walked two blocks to the Liberty Bell. When all the players and parents had gathered, Coach Pepper spoke. "We've got a few hours before we head to the field, so let's start the day with a little history." Coach swept his hand toward the Liberty Bell. "Anyone know why that bell is the most popular attraction in Philadelphia?"

"I don't know, Coach," Fivehead said, "but check out that big crack in the bell. It reminds me of Red Peters' head."

Coach put up a hand to quell the laughter. Then Ben spoke. "The Liberty Bell is popular because it symbolizes freedom."

Coach nodded. "Pretty good, Kwan."

"What's the bell made of?" Fivehead asked.

"Mostly copper and tin," Coach said, "with small bits of silver and gold."

"Who made the bell?" Max asked.

"Two craftsmen – John Pass and John Stow," Coach said. "Their names are on it."

"How did it crack?" Max asked.

Fivehead had an answer. "They ring it whenever I score a goal. That's why it's cracked."

Coach eyed Fivehead. "No more cracks out of you, Wesley."

Coach went on. "The bell was rung to celebrate important occasions. It was last rung in the year eighteen forty-six, at a birthday celebration for George Washington. That's when the crack got so bad that they stopped ringing it."

"George Washington, wasn't he a famous striker?" Fivehead joked.

Coach dug into his pocket, pulled out a dollar bill and a quarter, and held up one in each hand. "George Washington is one of only three presidents to have his image on both a coin and a paper bill."

Fivehead took a close look at the bill. "Coach, didn't they have barbers in those days? I mean, George looks like he was the lead singer in a rock band."

The boys snickered. "It was a different era, Wesley," Coach said. "People dressed differently, they wore their hair differently."

Coach checked his sheet. "Okay, time for

some extra credit. Who can name the two other presidents on both a coin and a bill?"

Ben put up a hand. "Abraham Lincoln and Thomas Jefferson."

"You're on fire, Ben!" Coach raved. "Lincoln is on the penny and the five-dollar bill. Jefferson is on the two-dollar bill and the nickel."

Coach led the team up the street, where he pointed to a brick building. "That's the President's House. George Washington and John Adams, our first two presidents, both lived there." Max raised a hand. "But Coach, the president lives in Washington D.C."

"Philadelphia was our nation's capital for ten years," Coach explained. "After that, the capital was moved to Washington."

Fivehead raised a hand. "Coach, this is a blast, but I'm gettin' hungry."

"Four more blocks, Wesley. Come on, let's check out the first American flag."

"I know about the flag," Fivehead whined. "Red, white and blue, stars and stripes, let's eat."

Coach ignored Fivehead and walked up to a house made of red brick, a flag flying off its roof. "Anybody know who lived here?" Coach asked.

"Betsy Ross," Ben said. "She made the first American flag."

"Ben, how do you know all this stuff?" Coach asked.

"My mom gave me a book about Philadelphia," Ben said.

Coach pointed at the flag. "Max, how many stars on that flag?"

Max quickly counted the white stars, arranged in a circle. "Thirteen."

"That's right," Coach said. "Why thirteen stars and not fifty?"

"That flag was made in seventeen seventy-six," Ben jumped in. "Back then, there were only thirteen states."

"Very good!" Coach said. "Okay, double extra credit for this one. Anyone know why Betsy Ross was chosen to make the first flag?"

"She made ruffles for George Washington's shirts," Ben said.

"Wait a minute," Fivehead cut in. "Why did she make potato chips for George Washington's shirts?"

Coach smirked at Fivehead. "Can it, you

knucklehead. Ben's right. A ruffle is a kind of fabric. It makes a sleeve look puffy."

The boys walked a few more blocks to a huge building. "That's Independence Hall," Coach said. "That's where they signed the Declaration of Independence, making America a free country."

After another few blocks, the team reached the City Tavern. "This place is famous because George Washington ate lunch here often," Coach said.

Fivehead fired away again. "Lemme guess, Coach. His wig is hanging on the wall."

Coach lunged for Fivehead but he jumped away. The Thunder and their families settled in for lunch. Max gobbled a turkey club sandwich along with a pile of cole slaw. As he finished his last bite, Fivehead elbowed him. Max watched as Fivehead took a red pepper out of his salad bowl and dropped it into his water glass. When the pepper reached the bottom, Fivehead looked at Max. "You know what that means? Red is goin' down today."

Max held up his palm, and Fivehead slapped it. On the way out, Coach pointed to a picture of Benjamin Franklin. "Ben Franklin was an awesome inventor – the lightning rod, the iron stove, the odometer, even swim flippers."

"Swim flippers?" Fivehead echoed. "You mean the kind Red Peters uses when he does laps in his bathtub?"

The boys howled. Ben stuck up his hand. "Ben Franklin was also a writer, musician, and scientist."

Coach shot Ben a look. "Okay, Ben, now you're showing up the tour guide."

But Ben wasn't done. As the team walked back to the parking garage, he pointed to a tree standing in the center of a courtyard. "That's a hemlock," Ben said. "It's the state tree."

Fivehead shook his head. "Ben, you're a walking encyclopedia. What's the state ice cream?"

"Strawberry."

"You serious?"

Ben laughed. "Made that one up."

A bit later, Fivehead turned to Max. "Philadelphia is pretty cool. And I thought it was only famous for its cream cheese."

Max chuckled. "Fiver, you're a crack-up. You'll be on TV some day."

"Hope so," Fivehead replied. "Hey, all I

know is, there's nothin' funny about what we're about to do to Red Peters."

Max nodded. *Gonna play my best today, I can feel it.*

CHAPTER 14
REMATCH: THUNDER VS. LIGHTNING

U NDER A BLUE SKY AT three o'clock, Max
Miles and Red Peters came face to face
in the circle. Max put out his hand. Red
didn't move. The ref glared. "Shake his hand, or
I'll call out your coach." Red put out his hand,
but looked over his shoulder. The ref stuck a
finger at him. "I've got my eye on you, son."

With that, Red fixed his eyes on Max. Max
stared back, not one blink. *He's trying to psyche
me out, won't work today*. Max won the coin toss
and jogged back to the huddle. Coach Pepper
ran his eyes across every player, stopping on
Max. "Boys, this teams cheated us once, let's
go get some revenge." Coach put out a hand
and the boys made a stack. "Three, two, one,
THUNDER!"

Four minutes in, Lightning middie Billy Ford threw down the line into Eddie Hazard's path. Red glanced at the ref, who had his eyes on Eddie. Then Red stepped on the edge of Max's boot and took off for the box. "Now!" Red yelled. Eddie delivered a crisp pass onto Red's boot, Max scrambling to catch up. As Red neared the arc Chipper stepped up, but Red cut past him into the box. As Red cocked his leg, Max slid for the ball. He got all leg and no ball, slicing Red down hard. The whistle blew. The ref ran up and pointed at the penalty spot. He took out his book and held a yellow card over Max.

"Dangerous tackle, son," the ref said. "Do it again, and I'll send you off."

Red got up and patted Max on the hip. "I'll take this one, Max."

Max backed out of the box, his heart pounding. Red put the ball on the spot. Theo took his stance, bouncing left and right. Red stepped up and smashed a rocket high into the corner. Lightning 1, Thunder 0. Red broke into a sprint up the sideline, his teammates chasing him. Nearing the Thunder bench, he dropped to his knees and slid to a stop six feet from Coach Pepper. "Lightning rules!" Red shouted.

Back in the circle, Fivehead edged up to Max. "I saw Red step on your cleat. This is war, Max."

Max nodded. "Just get me the ball."

A bit later, Fivehead fed Max in the circle. Feeling Red on his shoulder, Max dummied through his legs and spun around Red. Eddie swung over, but Max blew past him. Out of nowhere, Red swooped in and clipped the ball off Max's boot. Red tapped to Eddie and took off. Eddie floated the ball into Red's path. Red collected at full speed, Max two yards behind. As Charlie neared, Red cut inside. Charlie and Max hit Red from both sides, and Red spilled into the grass.

Max saw the ref reaching for his book. *Oh no, he's gonna toss me!* The ref pulled out a yellow card, and held it over Charlie. Max blew out a sigh. He looked over at his dad. Mr. Miles pushed his hands toward the ground. Max nodded. *I'm trying to do too much.*

Red lined up the free kick, thirty yards out. He lashed a liner that sizzled straight at Theo. Theo caught it against his chest, the force of the shot knocking him on his heels. As Theo threw to Fivehead out wide, Max made a run up the flank. Fivehead tried to hit him, but Eddie got a boot in. Eddie gathered the ball and sprang past Fivehead. Max was caught up the field. Eddie fed Red in the middle and bolted for goal.

Red dribbled wide toward the corner of the box, opening a lane for Eddie to cut behind him. As Chipper and Artie closed on Red, he slid a no-look pass into Eddie's path near the arc. Eddie ran on and lashed a low laser. Theo dove. The ball sailed past him, struck the far post, and caromed across the goalmouth. Red had followed the shot. He beat Chipper to the loose ball and thumped in into the open net.

For a second time, Red took off for the Thunder bench. This time he slowed, raised his arms, and locked eyes with Coach Pepper. In the stands, Mrs. Miles sat on her hands. "Red Peters is too good, they can't stop him."

"Bad attitude, Mom," Betsy snapped back.

A bit later, the Thunder jogged off at halftime down two goals. Coach Pepper took off his cap and ran a hand over his bristles. "We're just lumping the ball around," he whined.

"Nobody's open," Artie fired back.

"Artie's right," Coach agreed. "Let's wake up, show for each other!"

Two minutes into the second half, Max gave the Thunder a spark. He swept up a loose ball, led Ben toward the corner, and broke for the box. Ben collected and thumped a long ball across the pitch. Max beat Red to it in the top corner of the box. Red took his stance between Max and the goal and tapped his hands together. "Bring it on, punk," Red sniped.

Out of the corner of his left eye, Max saw Chipper running free toward the arc. Max tapped to his right and cocked his leg, but then he slid the ball back into Chipper's path. Chipper ran on and cracked a bolt. The keeper froze. The ball whistled past him and snapped the net in the far corner.

The Thunder huddled around Chipper. "We're back in it!" Max yelled.

But the hill got steeper. The Lightning moved a fifth player to the back line. Each time the Thunder posed a threat, they met a wall of defenders. After yet another Thunder foray crumbled near the box, Max looked to the sideline. Mr. Miles held up both index fingers. *Eleven minutes left. Plenty of time.*

A bit later Eddie led Red down the flank, Max on him tight. Red collected and tried to beat Max, but Max met him with a crunching tackle. As the ball rolled over the line, Red glared at Max. "Touch me again boy, and I'll step on your face." Max smiled inside. *Good, I've got him rattled.*

When Fivehead won a loose ball a minute later, Max darted into an open seam and called out, "Fiver!" Fivehead fed Max, who built speed toward the box. Red lagged five yards behind. "Get Miles!" he shouted.

As a defender neared, Max decided he was close enough to unload. From twenty five yards he swung into a thunderous crack. The keeper dove, but the ball knuckled over his hands and punched the roof of the net. Thunder 2, Lightning 2. His chest going *boom-boom-boom*, Max turned and ran toward his bench. His teammates piled on, and Max spoke. "This is our game, boys, let's do it now!"

But Red had a few more tricks in his bag. He took the kickoff from Eddie, tapped through Max's boots, and dribbled toward Artie. Red scissored over the ball. Artie staggered onto his heels, and Red shot by. He neared the box alone, Max closing the gap. Theo came out, but Red cut around him. As Red cocked his leg to shoot at the open frame, Max lunged. He got a boot on the ball and then sliced Red to the turf. The ball rolled inches wide of the post.

Red sprang up and ran at the ref. "That's a penalty! That's his second card!"

"Clean tackle, ball first!" the ref shot back.

Chipper rose high and headed Eddie's corner kick out of the box. Ben ran it down and dribbled into an open lane on the flank. Max took off. Red matched his first few strides, but his tank was nearly empty. Red looked at the ref, who had his eyes on Ben. Red and Max locked eyes. Then Red snuck a short elbow into Max's side.

"Ahhh!" Max yelped as he sank to the grass. The ref looked over and saw his linesman waving his flag. He whistled play to a stop, ran over, and huddled with his assistant. As Max got to his feet, the ref jogged over to Red. He pulled out his book and took out a card, a red card.

Red's mouth hung open. "I didn't touch him!"

"You elbowed him."

"It was only a shoulder!"

"My assistant saw it, now get off!" the ref snapped.

Red jogged slowly off, giving Max time to shake off the pain. Max looked at his dad, who held up one finger. *Gotta do it now.*

Fivehead played the free kick to Chipper, who whacked a long ball ahead of Ben toward the corner. As Ben ran it down, Max took off for the box. Eddie grabbed his shirt, but Max swatted the arm away. Ben crossed, the ball curling in slightly behind Max. Max let instinct take over. He slowed, turned his back to goal, and leaped. Leaning back parallel to the ground, Max whipped his left leg up and lashed his right boot at the ball. '*Thump!*'

I hit that good, Max thought as he put out his hands to cushion his fall. His eyes away from goal, Max saw Chipper sink to his knees, his hands on his head. There was silence for a second, and then the crowd erupted. Max rolled over to see the keeper's face in the grass, the net draped over the ball.

Max didn't see it, but his bicycle kick had looped over the keeper and slipped under the bar. The keeper had never moved. He'd never seen a player shoot with his back to goal. Max got up and bolted into a sprint. As he neared the Thunder bench, he dropped into a slide. Soon he disappeared under a pile of teammates. "Best goal I've ever seen!" Fivehead wailed.

The ref blew his whistle, but the Thunder kept on celebrating. Finally, the ref put the ball down in the circle. "Thunder, get in position!" Coach Pepper yelled. "He's putting the ball in play!"

The ref blew his whistle again to start play. Max and his teammates sprinted back out, but Billy had already tapped to Eddie. As Theo neared, Eddie took one more touch and fired from thirty yards at the empty goal. Max watched the ball sail toward the net. *It's going in.* Eddie aim was perfect, but he had a bit too much boot. The ball hit the bar and dropped a few feet from the line.

The race was on, Eddie versus Theo. Eddie edged ahead. Nearing the ball, he swung his leg back. Theo dove. His fist and Eddie's foot came together at the ball. It trickled inches wide of the post. The ref blew his whistle, twice. Game over. Thunder 3, Lightning 2.

Theo tried to get up but Max tackled him and

the Thunder piled on. Finally, they jogged to the bench and huddled around Coach Pepper. "My word for the day is 'GRIT,'" Coach said. "It means 'toughness.' You got down two, but you never quit, you showed your grit. Come on, let's shake their hands."

Max got in line. The third player he met was Eddie. "Nice game," Max said. Eddie shook, but he couldn't talk over the lump in his throat. At last, Max met Red. "Miles, you won today, but you know I'm better than you," Red snapped.

Max stared into Red's watery eyes. "My team won, Red. That's all I care about."

Red had no response. He turned and slinked off. Max walked over to his family. His dad gave him a bear hug. "That's the best half you've ever played, Max."

"Thanks, Dad."

Betsy put out her fist and Max bumped it. "Max, your bicycle kick, no keeper coulda saved that."

"Thanks, Bets. Guess all those kicks on the trampoline paid off."

Mrs. Miles gave Max a hug. "How does it feel to beat Red Peters?"

"Feels great. After he elbowed me, I knew we were gonna win."

As Max and his family neared the lot, a familiar figure approached. Gary Ball put out a hand, and Max shook it. "Tremendous game, Max, you made the difference."

"Thanks," Max said.

"Could we talk for a minute?" Coach Gary asked.

Max nodded, and he followed Coach Gary over to the corner flag. Coach looked Max in the eye. "You know that email I sent last month, well, forget it," Coach said. "I saw a different player today. You worked harder than anyone. You controlled the game with your passing. And your bicycle kick, any pro would've been proud of that."

Max smiled, and Coach Gary went on. "So here's the deal, Max. I want you on my state team."

Max felt his jaw drop. "But Coach, you said your team was set?"

"I had one slot open," Coach Gary said. "I was planning to offer it to Red Peters. But he just lost it, and you earned it."

Max was too numb to talk. Coach broke

the silence. "We have the best training, Max. We play the best competition, we even play overseas. Trust me, the Falcons will inspire you to become the best player you can be."

Max thought about Fivehead, and all the other friends he had made. He thought about how much he loved Coach Pepper. "I really like playing for the Thunder."

Coach Gary nodded. "I understand, Max. All I ask is that you think it over. Let me know by next Friday, okay?"

Max nodded. Coach put out his hand and Max shook it. Max watched him walk away. *Man, I got a big decision to make. But that's okay, because right now, I'm on top of the world.*

ACKNOWLEDGEMENTS

My parents, Bob and Dorothy Summers, took me to England at age six and introduced me to the greatest game on earth.

Laurie Summers, my dear spouse, read the manuscript countless times and made it better on each turn.

My children, Kate, John, and Caroline, provided helpful editorial insights. Kate also drew a fine illustration that served as the basis for the cover art.

My brother, Rob, and his spouse, Corie, were a source of steady encouragement. A special thanks to their daughters, Kaia Summers and Ruby Summers. Kaia and Ruby read the manuscript, asked lots of thoughtful questions, and even pointed out a few errors. Their reaction alone made writing the book worthwhile.

ABOUT THE AUTHOR

Bill Summers is a soccer author, journalist, player, and coach. He is the author of the Max Miles Soccer Series for boys, made up of *Clash of Cleats*, *Cracked Cleats* (coming soon), and *Comeback Cleats* (coming soon). Summers has also written the Shannon Swift Soccer Series for girls, featuring *Magic Boots*, *Scuffed Boots* (coming soon), and *Buffed Boots* (coming soon). He is the author of the young-adult novel, *Red Card*. His book on coaching, *The Soccer Starter*, was published by McFarland & Company. As a parent, Summers coached boys' and girls' youth teams for over a decade. He was captain of the men's soccer team at Cornell University, where he earned his degree in Communication Arts. To learn more, visit www.billsummersbooks.com.

Made in the USA
San Bernardino, CA
15 October 2018